WHEN WA|

LAUNDRY COTTAGE

By Sarah Colliver

Cover designed by Emma Gazzard

This is a complete work of fiction, including character, locations & scenarios.

All rights reserved.

Sarah Colliver 2024

This book is for all those we have loved,

lost, and carry within our hearts.

For me, sadly, the list is long.

But a special mention to

Jane Humm

who brought laughter and honesty to the table, and who in my early days of writing, believed in me.

LAUNDRY COTTAGE:

The Price family of Linton spent many years living in Laundry Cottage, with their mum and gran. Their wonderful tales of sisterhood, and of family escaping from the bombs of London, inspired me to name Aunty Violet's cottage this way.

WHEN WAR CAME TO LAUNDRY COTTAGE by Sarah Colliver

Before her arrival

Her aching feet pounded the familiar route to the factory. Despite the lack of street lighting, due to the blackout, she knew every turn and path, and thought she could even manage it with her eyes closed. She was late again, and this time Mr Graham would not be so understanding. Her excuses were running out and his patience thin. Everyone had a reason to be rushing around, the war was disruptive. Road closures, air raids, queuing for measly rations. Nothing could be done quickly it would seem, and inevitable late arrivals were impossible to avoid.

She examined the sky for the approaching rumble. Where was the air raid siren? With wide eyes, she wondered if it were true what they said, that the bomb which would kill you, had your name on it. The siren screamed his warning, but it was too late already, and her shaking legs rooted her to the pavement. Frozen, all she could do was stare, as the bombs hurled towards the earth only a few streets from where she stood. The ground shook with each explosion. Buildings around her rattled and groaned.

WHEN WAR CAME TO LAUNDRY COTTAGE by Sarah Colliver

She flung her hands over her ears and crouched as close to the ground as she could, as glass shattered around her.

When she finally stood up and dusted herself off, checking briefly for injury, she decided to make a dash for it, and sneak into the shelter to sit out the rest of the raid. She took a deep breath and ran. Mr Graham would be far too distracted to notice her arrive, and she could pretend to have been there all along.

Rounding the corner by the Post Office, she sped through the alley towards the back entrance of the factory, which she planned to slip in through. But acrid smoke belching into the air, halted her arrival, as fierce flames devoured the building, her factory. Fire engine bells began to ring chaotically, and streams of water fought to overcome the angry fire. It was a direct hit, and with all the materials inside, would be reduced to a pile of rubble and ashes in no time. Guilt crept into her mind, as she acknowledged her wish for divine intervention to avoid a ticking off. She hadn't meant for this to happen and made a mental note to be incredibly careful what she wished for in future. Lateness had saved her life, and that bomb wasn't

WHEN WAR CAME TO LAUNDRY COTTAGE by Sarah Colliver

meant for her. Overwhelmed, with mixed emotions, she approached the exhausted firemen, to see if there was anything she could do.

She mouthed offerings up to the God in the sky, that her fellow workers made it to the shelter in time, but the delayed air raid siren meant they were likely all dead. Her legs threatened to buckle, as a fireman shouted, "Get back girl, let us do our job! The all clear hasn't sounded yet! Head to the nearest shelter!"

She staggered backwards, away from the brave man, who looked drained; his face glistening with sweat and tinged with soot and ash. Her saucer eyes, almost blind with tears, watched the devastating scene unfold. Any fear of further bombs was clouded by the horror which consumed her, as they began to pull bodies from the rubble, and she wanted to scream, but her voice remained silent. A firm pull on her arm, from a woman whose uniform bore fresh stains from her busy shift, wrenched her away into a waiting ambulance.

"What's your name love? Can you hear me? I think you're in shock, you need a hot sweet tea. Come on, this way."

Sybil said nothing and allowed this kind stranger to guide her somewhere else, anywhere away from the chaotic destruction. How many hours had she worked in that building? How often had she gone home with sore feet from standing on the cement floor of that factory? The floor, which was now reduced to rubble and buried beneath tons of debris. She should have been in that building, beneath that wreck.

ONE

Sybil inhaled deep breaths as she fought the urge to vomit. The bus seemed devoid of any suspension and exacerbated her travel sickness. She preferred the gentle motion of trains with their familiar plumes of smoke, rickety-rick rhythm, and cocoon-like carriages. Her current method of transportation was bone shakingly exhausting. She checked her watch and

WHEN WAR CAME TO LAUNDRY COTTAGE by Sarah Colliver

sighed. Still three hours to go until arrival. She had visited only once as a child, when her parents had helped with the hop picking, but her memories were vague. She pulled out her compact from a worn leather handbag and powdered her paled face.

"Excuse me, could I borrow that for one moment?" A well-spoken voice drew louder and arrived next to her, on the empty seat. "It's just I have a pip stuck in my tooth, see?" She drew her lips open and displayed her rows of straight perfect teeth.

Sybil laughed. "Here, be my guest."

"Thanks so much. It's been driving me mad. My sister must have pinched my compact before I left."

"I'm Sybil."

"Harriet. You're a darling, can I call you Sybbie?"

"If you like. Where are you headed?" Sybil could not determine. She wasn't dressed in any uniform, and nothing gave her destination away.

"Dewton. Someone my father knows, needs a nanny. It was to stop me signing up really, but I haven't ruled

WHEN WAR CAME TO LAUNDRY COTTAGE by Sarah Colliver

that out...I promised to give this a try first. Anyway, she is desperate for help, and company apparently. Her frightful husband, is playing war all the time."

Sybil's face squashed in confusion. "Playing war?"

"Oh! What I mean is, he has a comfortable number with the government, so he uses his position to be in London all the time, but my mother saw him with his floozy. And that is really what keeps him so 'busy.' To pacify his wife, I am to be her 'companion,' but under the guise of a nanny. It's more like a sacrificial lamb, being packed off to the back of beyond!"

"I see." Sybil could not take her eyes off Harriet.

"You? You aren't dressed as a land girl, no uniform. Let me guess...escaping the bombs? Chasing after a lost love? Running away?"

"Nothing that exciting I'm afraid. I am staying with my aunt, her sight is beginning to fail, and her son is away fighting. My uncle Cyril died in the first war, so my dad has arranged for me to spend a few months with her, helping with the chickens, garden, housework, that kind of thing." For the first time, now she verbalised

WHEN WAR CAME TO LAUNDRY COTTAGE by Sarah Colliver

what lay ahead, she realised she was about to become a housewife to an aged woman. Her heart sunk a little.

"Sounds as if your dad is spiriting you away from the bombing and ticking off a few life lessons for you too. What a clever man."

Sybil shuddered. On arriving home, after the factory bombing, she found her house in mourning. The grapevine was speedy in their part of town, and within an hour, word got back to her mum about the direct hit. Convinced that Sybil was at work when the bomb struck, the house was thrown into premature grief. When Sybil silently entered the kitchen, where everyone had gathered, neighbours and all, it was as though they had seen a ghost. For a moment, the room hushed, and everyone stared at her with paled faces. The eerie silence soon erupted with screams and wails of relief.

Harriet continued to chatter, oblivious to Sybil's distracting thoughts. "How old are you? No, let me guess, seventeen?"

WHEN WAR CAME TO LAUNDRY COTTAGE by Sarah Colliver

"Nearly 18."

"Well, I turn twenty-one next month. Things can change then, but for now, I'll have a go at this 'companion' idea and enjoy some country living. Do you have a boyfriend?"

"Sort of, nothing firm, but he is overseas. We try and write regularly but…"

"Who knows what'll happen, it's uncertain times isn't it? I am trying not to be tied up with any one man, I only want to enjoy today. But if Mr Right walks through that door and sweeps me off my feet…" She gave a dramatic sigh and closed her eyes for a second, as though she were imagining the scenario.

Harriet was a whirling dervish. Sybil had never met anyone quite like her before. Her strawberry hair was pinned into smooth rolls, and she wore tiny diamond studs in her ears. A sweep of blush coloured her cheeks, and her red lips were perfectly drawn into peaks. Something about her was magnetic and it was at that moment Sybil knew, that they would be friends.

WHEN WAR CAME TO LAUNDRY COTTAGE by Sarah Colliver

"Shall we exchange addresses? Might be nice to have a friend Sybbie, when we are both so far away from home. Perhaps if we get any time to ourselves, we can meet up? Are you in Dewton too?" Harriet was already scribbling. She tore off a sheet, handed it to Sybil, then held out the notebook. "Here, write yours down too."

"I am staying near Dewton, about a ten-minute walk apparently." Sybil wrote down her details.

"Oh, that's great news. See, we haven't even arrived yet and we already have each other."

Sybil smiled. Harriet seemed warm and friendly, it would be nice to have someone closer in age, to reach out to, because she was bound to get homesick. Her two closest friends had been killed. They were better at timekeeping than Sybil, and had arrived on time that fateful day, doomed to be flattened by a Nazi bomb. She swallowed her wandering thoughts away and Phillip arrived instead. She felt guilty that she didn't miss him, but they had only enjoyed a short time together before he was posted away, barely time to know if they were even compatible. Sometimes she

WHEN WAR CAME TO LAUNDRY COTTAGE by Sarah Colliver

wondered if she was still writing to him out of compassion, rather than in a romantic way. How could you break it off with someone when their life was in danger and may never come home? It was fine for the time being, whilst she was single, but their letters were less romantic as time went on. It was probably comforting to receive news from home, regardless of how deep the connection went, and this is what spurred her on to continue.

"Right. That's decided then. Does your aunt have a telephone? You haven't put a number down?"

"No, but there may be one nearby I can use."

"Great, so you telephone me when you can, and we will arrange our first meet up, when we have both found our feet in our new positions. Isn't it funny, how things turn out. I was livid about being forced to get this bus here, wanted a car to bring me, but Daddy refused, and now I'm so glad he did, because we would never have met, would we? So, you must get in touch, and we can have fun together." She winked.

WHEN WAR CAME TO LAUNDRY COTTAGE by Sarah Colliver

It sounded more of an order than a question, but Sybil didn't mind. Harriet was an organiser it seemed, and sometimes that was a blessing, because it meant things would happen. And judging by the lack of villages the further they drove, she was going to need something more than being a country housewife to an old lady.

TWO

The moonlit scurry to the outhouse, wasn't too bad in the long sunny days, but how she would manage in the winter months, when the crisp air was deathly cold, she dreaded to think. The neatly cut up newspaper, was one of her jobs now, and her aunt insisted they be uniform, 'we may not have an inside privy, but we can still maintain our standards,' she would say. This made Sybil laugh. The journey on the bus two weeks before, seemed to have carried her back in time, rather than to the countryside. Everything seemed so much slower, and even simple

WHEN WAR CAME TO LAUNDRY COTTAGE by Sarah Colliver

tasks took longer. Laundry Cottage was quaint and pretty but lacked the more modern comforts of her city home. They still used the tin bath in front of the fire, and water was drawn from a well in the garden. Although this was time consuming, and labour intensive, there was something deliberate about these tasks, and she was surprised about how quickly she adjusted.

She dropped the latch on the lavatory door, and the bright moon drew her to the front gate, where a delicate pink rose bush draped elegantly along the dry-stone wall. High hedges, teaming with wildlife, lined the country lane where Laundry Cottage sat. It was picture perfect and seemed incomprehensible that people stared up at the same sky as her, and yet faced danger and tyranny where they stood. She imagined what conflict the moon must feel, as he watched over the fractured world, seeing beauty where she stood, simultaneously, with the grotesque images of people being blown to bits. She shuddered and shook away the image of the factory, and the injured faces of her friends. Her ears replayed the familiar wail of the air-raid siren, were her parents

WHEN WAR CAME TO LAUNDRY COTTAGE by Sarah Colliver

safe? Her stomach churned and she remembered what Harriet had said, about how clever her dad had been, 'spiriting' her away to safety. Gratitude washed over her and as she wiped away fresh tears, she crossed her fingers for her parents and muttered a quiet prayer up to the sky.

Once settled back into bed, she decided to wander along to the telephone box in the morning, to call Harriet; arrange to meet. Distraction from her dark thoughts could be just the thing she needed.

Sybil checked her watch, Harriet was late. She leant against the wall of the church hall, beneath the shade of an old oak. The heavy string bags rubbed her hands, and she was glad to put them down. Perhaps she should have shopped after their meeting.

"Sybbie!" The cheery greeting jolted Sybil from her thoughts, and she was enveloped in a warm hug before she could answer.

"Harriet, how lovely to see you again." She wanted to moan about how long she had been waiting, but was instantly distracted by the picnic hamper, which stood beside her feet.

"I brought lunch. There's nowhere decent to get anything here, unless you want to sit with the WI ladies and enjoy a scone masquerading as a rock cake. Really Sybbie, I almost lost my teeth! There were some sweet old dears in there, but it's not really my scene, nor yours I should think. I'm sure you are ready for the company of someone below the age of thirty-five. So, here is the best luncheon two girls could dream of these days."

Sybil marvelled at how much Harriet seemed to cram into her sentences, and before she could answer, was lugging her shopping bags down a shady pathway behind the church, trying to keep up.

"There is the most beautiful view this way, and a perfect place for us to sit, whilst we catch up. Now tell me, is it as frightful as you imagined?"

Sybil considered the question. "Well, it's not frightful. It isn't altogether exciting either, but it's nice to know I can help Aunty Vi. She fusses me in her own way.

WHEN WAR CAME TO LAUNDRY COTTAGE by Sarah Colliver

That helps stave off the home sickness. Never thought I would miss city life...my poor eyes cannot get used to the oil lamps, sometimes we even resort to the candles."

"It's not much further. Follow me, through here." Harriet pushed a prickly bush and held it up for Sybil to duck under. "Bloody thorns! Ouch! Here see, it's worth the pain, take a look!"

As described, a small bench sat at the top of a steep incline, and as far as the eye could see, was a patchwork of fields and valleys framed by an endless sky.

"Sit here, and catch your breath, isn't it beautiful? Now, what's this about candles?"

"Oh, and we have an outside privy too..."

Harriet's steely eyes stared for a moment before she broke into laughter. "You unfortunate thing! Next, you'll be telling me that you use newspaper too!"

Sybil blushed. Her tummy grumbled. Their diet was sufficient, more so than living off the measly rations back home, in the city. But there were still limitations to what was on offer, compared to pre-war days. Often Aunty Vi would make lettuce sandwiches with a pinch of salt for lunch, which tasted as boring as it sounds. She was frugal, had a seemingly never-ending supply of them, and they seemed to be her speciality. Curiosity and excitement crept up to her lips, and she licked them in anticipation as Harriet purposefully undid the leather straps on the basket, and handed her two plates.

"How does ham and mustard sandwiches, pork pie, and scones with jam and cream sound?"

"Delicious, thank you so much." Sybil tucked into her generous plate of food, and only after several mouthfuls became aware of Harriet barely nibbling the edge of a sandwich. "Aren't you hungry too?"

"Had a huge breakfast. Perhaps your aunt would like mine?"

Sybil fought the pride which may prevent her accepting the food. It was one thing to share a picnic with someone, something altogether different to be taking it home. But she could imagine the look of delight on Aunty Vi's face, at the scones, and felt guilty that she hadn't even spared her a single thought whilst shovelling in her food. "Thank you, I know she would love that." Sybil accepted graciously, but unease pecked at her tummy, although it could have been the rich food she was not used to eating.

THREE

Sybil stretched out her arms and stood up with a groan. She only intended to pull up a few dandelions for the rabbits, but three hours later, and deep in thought she had weeded the entire area. Now her body begged for a break and her stomach groaned. It was gone one and Aunty Violet's cheery humming grew closer.

"Tea and sandwiches for my favourite niece. Ooh and we have a special treat for supper later, I've been stewing apples!"

WHEN WAR CAME TO LAUNDRY COTTAGE by Sarah Colliver

Sybil smiled and hopped up onto the coal bunker, wiping her hands on her patched cords. Her parched throat eased with her warm weak tea, and she felt revived.

"Not quite the feast we enjoyed last week. I shall dine out on that memory for a long time dear. Fresh cream and scones! How fancy! And how the other half live eh? Can't fault her for her generosity though, giving me her share." Aunty Vi's eyes always wept a little tear when she smiled, and she wiped it with the corner of her embroidered hanky. "Is your lettuce sandwich too salty?"

"It's delicious, thank you."

"The way you are sorting out my garden for me, we shall have enough lettuce to see us to the end of the war. God willing that comes by Christmas."

Sybil nodded and smiled, tight lipped from her full mouth, and because she was already sick of them, but her mother's voice came to mind and swiftly ticked her off, reminding her to be grateful for a full belly.

WHEN WAR CAME TO LAUNDRY COTTAGE by Sarah Colliver

"I forgot! Here, this is for you. Was on the doormat earlier when I went to sweep the front step. Look at that fancy handwriting, and no address, so whoever it is from must have dropped it off. Maybe it's your scones lady?"

Sybil took the pristine envelope with her blackened hands and placed it next to her.

"Aren't you going to read it then?"

Aunty Vi was more excited about the delivery than she was, so she put down her sandwich and opened it up. "Yes, you're right, it's from Harriet. Wants me to meet her again, dropped it off whilst taking the children for a bike ride."

"It's lovely that you have a new friend so soon and one so lively..."

Sybil wondered why her stomach sunk a little, to her aunt's positive statement. "Yes, I'm lucky. She wants to plan a party at the house, and I think this may involve me. Can't manage it all on her own."

WHEN WAR CAME TO LAUNDRY COTTAGE by Sarah Colliver

"Something to look forwards to, eh? Have you got anything suitable to wear to a fancy party?"

Sybil examined her scruffy clothes, turned over her dirtied hands and examined the soil wedged beneath her nails. She shrugged her shoulders and pulled a silly face. "You implying that I'm not good enough, just the way I am?" Sybil minced along the cobbled path, pouting and with her hand on her hip.

"Oh," Aunty Vi struggled to speak through her laughter, "you have brought this place back to life, haven't laughed like this in ages."

Sybil drew in her tiny aunt and hugged her close. "I'm happy to be here, with you."

"Well, I better dig up some of those potatoes, might be able to do a swap with Doris." Aunty Vi rolled up her sleeves.

Sybil scratched her head. "What do you mean?"

"Doris, young lass. Similar size to you I reckon. She has three young'uns to feed, reckon a basket of potatoes might tempt her to part with one of her frocks. She used to turn heads, that one. Her Bernard struck gold marrying her." Vi's words trailed behind her as she went in search of the garden fork, and a sack to fill.

Sybil leant against the fence, and drained the last of her tea, with a warm glow in her cheeks from her aunt's kindness. How lucky she was. It could have been a different story if Vi was a bitter old woman. It was almost as though having company was more important to her, than any of the practical stuff she could take on. Aunty seemed a little spritelier with each joke they enjoyed or hug they shared, and she no longer seemed like the decrepit old lady, who greeted her at the bus stop, and struggled to climb the hill home. She had a new spring in her step, and this made Sybil happy.

The long driveway to Deanwood House, stretched out beyond the sign, which sternly stated it was 'PRIVATE PROPERTY' and 'part of the Deanwood House Estate.' Despite her invite, Sybil felt like a trespasser as she trod the lengthy path. She cursed at the remaining dirt beneath her nails, which she had fought to remove with the wizened bristle nail brush, and repeatedly straightened her cardigan, praying that the darned hole remained hidden behind her peacock brooch.

A canopy of oaks lined the driveway, and closer to the house, smartly painted lampposts. Above the Tudor red bricked house, an array of tall chimneys stretched up to the sky. Countless delicate, leaded windows hinted at the many rooms contained within, and an ancient wisteria swept across the bottom of the wall and over the front door. Sybil gasped and felt as though she should be scurrying around the back, to wherever the servant entrance was located.

"Sybbie! I'll be right down!" Harriet called from an open window on the third floor and Sybil imagined her now running down the stairs, in her usual enthusiastic way. She burst through the heavy arched front door and wrapped herself around her. "It's wonderful that you're here! Come on, come in, we can have tea around the back on the lawn. It's divine in the afternoons. The sun is there and stays until it sets. I have a table all ready for us."

WHEN WAR CAME TO LAUNDRY COTTAGE by Sarah Colliver

Harriet closed the door behind them, and ushered her along a maze of panelled hallways, and on through what appeared to be a music room, with high ceilings and doors out into the garden. She could barely catch her breath, and her eyes fought to capture the detail and magnitude of the property, but within seconds, they were back outside and beneath the warm sun.

"See, didn't I tell you how magnificent it is out here. Over there is the tennis court, and round there we have our own maze, can you believe it? Further down is the lake, and round there, just around that corner, is the kitchen garden, and there is all sorts growing in there. Now, sit down. Let me give you a cushion. How do you take your tea? Sugar?"

Sybil's head reeled and struggled to keep up with everything that was said. She didn't know which direction to look first, but Harriet was right, whichever way you faced was a treat for the eyes.

"I'll put two lumps in, because frankly you look as though you need something sweet and Ward is finishing off our cake, so we shall have to wait for that

I'm afraid." She stirred in Sybil's sugar and handed her the cup and saucer.

"Thank you," were the only words which she could verbalise for the moment.

"So, now you're here, isn't this the perfect place for a party?"

Sybil sipped her sweet tea. "Is this a party for you or the lady who you work for?"

"For me, silly! She is away, in Devon with her sister for a couple of weeks. She even took the children and said I should stay here, keep an eye on the place. So, I am the lady of the house now."

"Won't she mind?"

"Well, she said I could entertain a few friends, and my 'few,' and her 'few,' may differ...but it is in honour of me finally getting the old 'key to the door,' so to speak!"

Sybil saw something flash in her friend's eyes. Was she testing her? "Oh yes, your twenty first! Of course."

WHEN WAR CAME TO LAUNDRY COTTAGE by Sarah Colliver

"So, you see, you must help me, I can't possibly do this all by myself. To begin with, we need to find out where all the young men hang out, and pay it a visit. A party without someone to dance with, wouldn't be worth throwing. There is a dance on, this weekend, at the Memorial Hall, and I have already taken the liberty of obtaining us tickets... and I know what you are going to say, that you have nothing to wear...but I already have a dress which I know you'll love. So that's that. Oh, and you must stay here afterwards, so we can dissect every detail together. I insist darling."

Sybil placed her cup on the table. It was all arranged, and despite feeling a little manipulated, the thought of music and dancing, ignited a fire within. "I'm in."

FOUR

Aunty Vi stood at the gate, and waved until Sybil turned the corner and was out of sight. Guilt remained at leaving her behind, but Sybil knew that she could regale her with tales of the dance on her return home, and they would chat about it for hours. Her bag was light, on account that her outfit was hanging up in Harriet's wardrobe, and so she only needed the essentials. Harriet insisted they get ready together and that they be driven to the village in style. Sybil acknowledged the butterflies she felt, which had been absent for so long, and her irrepressible enthusiasm powered her walk to the big house.

The driveway was less intimidating now she knew the owners were away, and she slammed the heavy knocker against the front door. Footsteps grew nearer on the other side and then the door swung open. "Yes?" A portly woman with a pristine white pinny stared at Sybil. Her stern face was pale and wrinkled.

"Hello. I'm here to see..."

"Sybbie! It's fine, thank you Ward, I shall take over now."

Ward closed the door behind them and disappeared without a sound.

WHEN WAR CAME TO LAUNDRY COTTAGE by Sarah Colliver

"Come on, up here." Harriet was already around the turn of the staircase and out of sight, as Sybil ran to catch up.

"Do you always do everything this quickly?" Sybil took two steps at a time.

Harriet stopped and turned, with a mischievous smile, "No darling, not *everything*."

Sybil knew what she implied and stifled a giggle as Harriet slipped in through a doorway.

"Here, put your bag down, and let's cheers, to us." She handed her a fizzing champagne flute. Sybil's wide eyes betrayed her thoughts. "First time? Well don't be put off, sometimes it takes a while to become accustomed to these things. Cheers."

Sybil sipped the golden liquid, and the bubbles tingled on her tongue. She didn't need to learn to like it at all, it was delicious. Giggly and relaxed, she padded around the room, in awe of the faces staring down at her from the ancient oil paintings, wondering what they thought about this lowly city girl, drinking fine champagne in their ancestral home. She raised her glass to them in thanks and laughed, before sprawling out on the four-poster bed.

"Don't get too comfortable darling, we need to make ourselves beautiful...we have plans to execute, work to do. Think of this as our guest list preparation. Cheers." Harriet drained her glass and then began to lay out a plethora of jewellery and make up, hair pins and scent. She had everything planned and all Sybil had to do was go along with it.

Sybil crossed her legs and tried to be as elegant as Harriet, who seemed to manage it effortlessly. When Harriet had finally allowed her to gaze in the full-length mirror, Sybil had gasped at her reflection. She felt like a film star. The glamourous woman staring back at her, was barely recognisable. Harriet had scalded her for crinkling her dress, when she threw her arms around her in gratitude, but she seemed proud of how Sybil had turned out and beamed. "Just look at you darling! Prepare for heads to turn tonight."

WHEN WAR CAME TO LAUNDRY COTTAGE by Sarah Colliver

Their driver opened the car door for them, and Harriet climbed out first, straightening her skirt and beaming at Sybil. The band were in full swing, and the fear of missed opportunities to dance, drew them quickly inside.

The hall was decorated with red, white and blue paper chains, peppered with tables and chairs around the edge and filled with excited chatter. The jolly saxophone enticed even the most reluctant dancers onto their feet and the floor throbbed with the enthusiastic feet pounding it. This was her first dance without Philip, and it was as though she had been holding her breath until this moment. She felt so alive. Within seconds they were pulled separately onto the dance floor and whirled around by uniformed partners. Her's was American and had slick, greased back hair and a packet of cigarettes in his top pocket. He pulled her close and held her tight- a little too 'handsy' for her liking.

The song ended. "Thank you, that was fun." Sybil turned and headed to the long trestle table, set up as a bar.

"Here, allow me." Her suitor followed close behind, with his hand on her back. "We'll take two beers."

"No, not for me thanks. I don't really like beer."

"Well honey, what do you like?" The soldier leant in a little too close, his eyes lingered on her breasts. She flinched and pulled back.

"It's fine, really, I can get my own, I'm with my friend. But thanks anyway." Sybil pushed through the throng of people and found Harriet, who was smoking a cigarette, surrounded by a group of GIs.

"Here she is, isn't she beautiful. Didn't I tell you? Sybbie, come and meet these gentlemen, all the way from America." She pulled her in and locked arms, as the soldiers whistled appreciatively. Sybil had never been in situations where people paid her attention before and was unsure how to handle it. She looked at Harriet, who stood tall and commanded the scene.

"Hello. You're all so handsome in your uniforms," she managed to shout above the music.

Harriet beamed at her approvingly. "Don't they! So, who's up for the next dance?"

A playful tussle erupted, but the more senior soldiers took their hands, pulling rank over their men. He was an older man, maybe thirty, and Sybil noticed his wedding ring. His green eyes spotted her stare. "I'm not hiding the fact. I could have taken it off before I came out, and no one would ever know. But I'm not doing anything wrong, a harmless dance, some female company. That's all." He smiled, and Sybil relaxed into his hold, assured he was after nothing more than a dance.

The room spun as he twirled her around and led her around the dancefloor with ease. Excitement bubbled through them both. Their instant connection was undeniable. It seemed odd, that strangers, with such few words exchanged, could be so synchronised. Before long the crowded floor cleared, and everyone clapped enthusiastically for them. Spurred on by their appreciation, Sybil lost herself, deep within his expert control, and her body seemed to know how to respond to his.

WHEN WAR CAME TO LAUNDRY COTTAGE by Sarah Colliver

As the final note played, he pulled her close, until his heavy breath pressed his chest against hers, and his eyes held her gaze. They stood motionless. With the crowd's cheers and whoops breaking their momentary spell, Sybil caught her breath and wiped her fallen curl away from her eyes, "Wow. You can certainly move!"

He smiled. "Would you like a drink?"

She looked around for Harriet, but she was on the edge of the dance floor, surrounded by willing suitors. "That would be lovely, thank you."

"What's your poison Ma'am?"

"A punch please."

"We'll have a punch and a beer, thank you."

Sybil took the glass from the soldier. "I don't even know your name."

"Walter Raslow. Pleased to meet you, But do me a favour and call me Walt? I always think I'm in trouble when people use my full name."

WHEN WAR CAME TO LAUNDRY COTTAGE by Sarah Colliver

"Well Walter, sorry, Walt! I'm Sybil Cooper. But you know that because my friend already told you."

"Your friend, she sure is…"

Sybil finished his sentence silently within her head: forward, bossy, overwhelming?

"Lively, I think that's the right word. May I say you are a surprisingly wonderful dancer yourself Sybil."

She couldn't ascertain if her flushed cheeks were from all the excitement or the compliment. "Only when I'm being led so confidently!"

His smile evaporated and his stare emptied. He was no longer in the hall, amidst the excitement of the band and cheerful chatter. His paled face was far away. "Are you alright Walt?"

His haunted expression gave Sybil the chills. She took the drink from his hand in fear it may fall to the floor and placed it on the nearest table with her own. Taking his hand, she led him towards the door into the fresh night air. There was a bench just beyond the post box, and she gently pressed him down to sit.

He stared up at the luminous moon. "Perfect for landing, bomber's moon."

Concern replaced Sybil's excitement, and she fought to untangle the words and what they implied. He had seen dark things, which left him at the mercy of his memories. That was evident. For a moment Philip sprung into her mind. Was he too haunted by things he had seen? She hadn't written to him since arriving at Aunty Vi's, and regardless of her feelings, she must continue to do so, some deep rooted, gut instinct told her this. She nodded to herself in acknowledgment.

Together they sat, quietly, with the thud of the band in the distance. It felt as though an hour passed, but it was more likely five minutes.

"Are you from around here?" His question confirmed he was back in the 'now.' Was he even aware of this strange trance episode?

"No, I am staying with my aunt. Are you alright?"

"Sure."

"You had a bit of a turn."

WHEN WAR CAME TO LAUNDRY COTTAGE by Sarah Colliver

Walt pushed a stick with the toe of his polished shoes and sighed.

"This bloody war. Ripping people away from their loved ones…" Sybil spoke softly.

"Honey, if that were all of my problems, I would be grateful…only…" He shook his head and pursed his lips. "I can't talk about it…"

He pulled out a pack of cigarettes and lit them both one. "Here."

Sybil accepted gratefully, and watched as Walt blew smoke from his nostrils like a dragon.

"You know, you need to be careful who you lead out here in the dark. Not all my comrades are as well intended as me, watch yourself."

Sybil drew on the cigarette. A warmth crept over her. Walt sounded like her dad, full of concern but he would not be impressed with her sitting alone with an American soldier, smoking. However, she felt safe with this one. "Thanks for the advice, I think I had kind of worked that out for myself a little earlier."

"Come on, let's go back inside. You should be dancing the night away, not sat out here with me." He threw his cigarette to the floor and grabbed her hand, "Let's show them what we can do eh?"

"Don't go to sleep Sybbie! So, Walter? Did you kiss him? You did, didn't you?" Harriet knelt on the bed next to her, resembling an excited child.

"NO! He is married."

"And? Since when was that a showstopper? We are at war you know; normal rules don't apply."

Sybil fought a gasp and shifted back to a more comfortable position. "Marriage does mean something, not everyone is sex mad you know!"

"Oh shush. While you were engaged with Walter, I managed to invite a plethora of men to our party, and I don't care if they are married or not. Is Walter coming along?"

Sybil scratched her head. "I forgot to ask him."

WHEN WAR CAME TO LAUNDRY COTTAGE by Sarah Colliver

Harriet's eyes narrowed, and her animated expression melted into anger. "You didn't even ask? That was the whole point of tonight!"

"You're angry with me?"

Harriet softened her tone, "No! Silly! But we were supposed to get the word out, that's all."

"You said you managed to invite loads of people. What difference does one make?"

Harriet slid off the bed and sat in front of the mirror, wiping off her makeup as she answered. "I'm sure he will hear about it anyway, from the others."

Why was she so focussed on Walt? But it was as though she could read her thoughts.

"You two were amazing dancing together, that's all. We could do with a bit of pizzazz at the party – get everyone dancing."

"It was as though we always dance together, it felt wonderful! I loved it. I suppose I could try and get a message to him. I could write him a note."

Harriet spun around and hopped back onto the bed. "Yes! Do it! First thing in the morning, we will write it and drop it over to his unit."

Harriet seemed more excited at the prospect of Walt attending than Sybil felt. But it would be lovely to dance with him again and she had never experienced that kind of attention before. Sybil yawned.

"Oh sleepyhead, you're no fun at all. I brought us up a little nightcap, to end our evening of fun. Come on we must toast, or we shall have terrible bad luck."

Sybil accepted the crystal brandy glass from her indulgent host, and they clinked glasses.

"To you, me, and the party of our dreams," Harriet toasted.

"Cheers!" Sybil sipped the brandy which burned her throat. She wouldn't get away without drinking it all and wondered if she would get used to it, the more sips she took. But she didn't and felt relief when the glass was empty.

WHEN WAR CAME TO LAUNDRY COTTAGE by Sarah Colliver

"I'm going to sleep here, next to you. It wouldn't be a proper sleepover otherwise, would it?" Harriet decided.

Sybil turned onto her side to face the looming portrait, whose shadowy features seemed to move. It spooked her at first, but she reasoned it was the light of the lamp coupled with her slightly tipsy vision.

Harriet turned out the light. "Night darling. Sleep tight."

"I brought you tea, and toast." Harriet placed a gilded tray on the vast bed and proceeded to open the curtains. "it's almost nine you know! I left you for as long as I could."

Sybil stretched and yawned, as she propped herself up with pillows behind her. "This is a treat. I've never had breakfast in bed before." Her sleepy mind acknowledged all the 'firsts' she was having since moving to the sleepy countryside. She could credit Harriet for making most of them happen.

"I popped a sugar in the tea for you, and there is a little pot of jam too, under that lid, should you want some. I dug this out as well." Harriet spun around and lifted a wooden box onto the bedside table, "it's got writing paper and envelopes inside."

Sybil sipped on her tea, marvelling at the boundless energy Harriet seemed to possess. "You have thought of everything it seems…thanks, I'll have a look when I've finished this. This food is delicious, thank you."

"Well, I thought it was best to strike while the iron is hot. No point wasting time, he might make other plans. And you are going to be very much on his mind this morning."

"You remember he is married? He made that clear to me Harriet. He isn't looking for anything."

"Hmmm. That's what he says, now. He is a long way from home darling. Men have needs. Why don't you start with: Dearest Walter, I was so pleased to have met you last night, and would absolutely love to dance with you again…"

WHEN WAR CAME TO LAUNDRY COTTAGE by Sarah Colliver

Sybil watched Harriet, as she dictated the letter, gliding around the room as though creating a work of fiction.

Harriet turned. "You haven't written a word. Come on, we haven't a moment to waste."

Sybil smiled and nodded, but decided to write her own words, and keep it friendly and not pushy. She licked the envelope and printed his name on the front before Harriet could read it and berate her. "Done."

"Good, now eat up and get ready then we can deliver it."

"Oh, I really must get back to Aunt Vi. I haven't got time today."

Harriet stared and then smiled. "Not a problem, I will get the driver to take me to the base and drop it off. Then I can get on with the planning. Have you got anything to wear to our party? It must be dazzling, as you and Walter are the star dancers!"

"Well, Aunty Vi was going to swap me a new dress, I say new, new to me anyway. So, it's taken care of..."

"Darling, you absolutely cannot throw on any old thing, I shall sift through my clothes and organise what you should wear. We simply must be the most beautiful vixens, have all those men drooling. And we had fun last night didn't we, getting ready together, so we must do it again, besides, you wouldn't ruin my birthday would you?"

Sybil stifled a sigh. It was fun, she couldn't argue with that and of course she would not want to ruin her birthday celebrations. But how she would decline Aunty Vi's kind gesture was beyond her. A rumbling in her tummy begged for jam and toast. Perhaps she would feel better and think clearer, once she had finished breakfast.

FIVE

Aunty Vi ran to the gate, eagerly awaiting her return home from the big house. "You never said you were a dancer... all around the village it is!" Sybil did not know how quickly news travelled around villages. And

WHEN WAR CAME TO LAUNDRY COTTAGE by Sarah Colliver

it seemed that both her dancing escapades, and the arrival of the beautiful Harriet, was the talk of local gossip. "You be careful, married he is, that GI. It isn't proper dancing with a married man, so far from home. Goodness knows what your father would say." She wagged her finger and her eyes narrowed. "Eh, fancy my own niece gracing Deanwood house, as an actual house guest. Were you up in the servant rooms?"

"No, I stayed in a four-poster bed, and I had breakfast in bed on a gold tray!"

"Never! I could only have found my way inside that place, using the back entrance, likes of me would never have been welcomed through the front, but to sleep in those bedrooms..." Aunty Vi's voice rose with excitement, and she soon forgot about the potential scandal of the married GI.

Sybil stacked the logs, which Norman had kindly delivered, ready for the approaching autumn. Norman lived on the next farm, and he and Aunty Vi looked out for one another. He often popped in with a rabbit, firewood, or some extra butter. Since they were both widowed, they helped each other out. He was a cheery and spritely man despite his age.

As she recalled her recent chatter with Aunty, she decided to be more discreet with her behaviour. It would break her heart to sully Aunt Vi's reputation, but dancing with Walt, was the biggest thrill of her life so far, and she genuinely felt no threat from him. It was as though they both understood it was platonic, nothing improper would evolve, regardless of what everyone looking-on, thought. His clouded mind was full of darkness, but the dancing seemed to distract his thoughts and his furrowed brow dissipated while the music played. Sybil suspected that it was his wife with whom he was dancing, locked in his own world, and she was simply the vessel. This was fine by her.

There was only a week until the party, and Harriet was in full operation party mode. The guest list was growing all the time, and who knew how much the whole thing was costing, and where the funding was coming from. For all Sybil knew, Harriet had a substantial income from her father. She should really take a gift with her but what could she possibly give

WHEN WAR CAME TO LAUNDRY COTTAGE by Sarah Colliver

Harriet, the woman who already has everything? Even Aunty Vi was at a loss. It would need to be a make do and mend. But the details still evaded her.

"Excuse me?" A smooth American accent jolted her from deep thoughts. The log she held dropped from her hand and landed on her foot. She yelped and hopped, supressing the profanity which attempted to spill from her mouth, and slumped on the front doorstep.

"I'm so sorry Ma'am, I didn't mean to startle you." The tall figure rushed to her aid and knelt in concern. His brown eyes, full of fear. "Are you ok?"

Sybil blushed and her eyes fluttered. "Oh, don't worry about me, I've been in much worse states. It wasn't your fault at all." She leaned to stand, and gratefully accepted his outstretched hand to steady herself. "Thank you."

He smiled. "Jeremiah Thomas, at your service." He removed his cap and nodded, without letting go of her hand.

"Sybil Cooper." Their mutual gaze lingered as her pain dissolved and excitement erupted. He stood about three foot taller, and his firm hand grip felt reassuring. It was as though he cast a spell, and in that moment, there was only them, despite the chaotic world which fought around them.

"That's a mighty pretty name, fitting I'd say." His velvet tone felt familiar, as though this voice was meant for her ears, and she fought the urge to draw him close and kiss him. Words failed her, as she drank in every inch of this stranger.

"I'm glad you're ok, Miss Sybil." He tucked his cap into his pocket, and smoothed back his shorn, black hair. "I was passing this way, and wondered if you could tell me how far and which way the village is?"

Sybil swallowed, unsure of this strange sensation, and wondering if he too felt this magnetic power. "Please call me Sybil."

"Well Sybil, since all the place signs have been removed, I could do with a point in the right direction."

WHEN WAR CAME TO LAUNDRY COTTAGE by Sarah Colliver

Sybil blinked herself out of her daze and smiled. "Please wait one moment. Don't move. Stay right here." She sped around the back of the house, oblivious to her newly swollen toe.

"Aunty Vi?" She ran into the cosy little sitting room, where Aunty Vi peacefully napped in the floral armchair. Sybil grabbed a piece of paper, and pencil from the drawer, and scrawled a note to explain she was nipping into the village. She could collect the fresh milk whilst there too and grab a stamp from the Post Office. After placing the note beside her sleeping aunt, she crept out to avoid waking her, hoping the handsome stranger was still waiting.

Jeremiah leant against the drystone wall at the front of the cottage, but stood up straight on seeing Sybil return. His face questioned her.

"I'm coming with you. I have milk to buy, so we can walk together."

He smiled. "Well, that's kind of you, but I'm not sure that's such a good idea."

Sybil's face dropped, and she searched his hands.

WHEN WAR CAME TO LAUNDRY COTTAGE by Sarah Colliver

"I'm not married, you looking for a ring?"

"First thing I check for these days. But what then? I'm single, you are a stranger to the area, like me really, because I'm not from around here either. They are a welcoming lot, although gossip about everything." She was already out of the gate and heading up the lane. "So, please, Jeremiah, let me show you the way."

He pulled his cap back onto his head, and within a couple of long strides, caught up with her. "If you're sure. Last thing I want is to bring anything to your door."

Sybil smiled. "Well, I'm truly glad it was my door you arrived at. When did you get here?"

"Two days ago, we're in the camp over the fields back there. Can't say a lot else, you know the old, 'careless talk costs lives' thing." He double tapped his nose with his fingertip and smiled. "'Mums the word', eh? Got the afternoon off, so thought I would explore."

"Do you get any other time off? I mean, my friend she is organising this party next week and I would LOVE it if you would come as my guest?"

WHEN WAR CAME TO LAUNDRY COTTAGE by Sarah Colliver

They strode along in silence with the question lingering in the air. Sybil convinced herself that she had misread the situation and cursed herself for being so forward. What on earth had come over her?

"I wish very much to accompany you to your friend's party."

Sybil beamed and her heart sped up.

"But, I must decline."

She stopped walking. It was as though her tangled thoughts had ensnared her feet, which could no longer move. "Right, sorry, I should never have asked, I mean we've only just met. You must think me very forward. I have never acted so impulsively before, you must believe me, I felt...never mind."

Jeremiah gently rested his hands on hers. "Hey," he whispered. "You have done nothing wrong. You are a fine young lady, and any man would be proud to have you stood next to him. But now, we must part ways, I have business to attend, and you have been kind enough to point me in the right direction. I hope to see you again, for a walk, maybe next time I'm passing?"

Sybil fought back her tears. Tears of rejection, embarrassment, and foolishness. She nodded and pursed her lips into a questionable smile.

He lifted her hand to his mouth and brushed his lips over it, before turning away from her and fast walking up the lane towards the village.

SIX

The antique armchairs in the library at Deanwood house, were Sybil's favourite place to relax, despite their worn appearance. She often wondered who had occupied them, over the years before. How they had dressed or how their lives played out. You could sense the history of the house at every turn and the eyes watching down from each looming portrait. Although relaxing was not usually the order of the day when in the company of Harriet, the rare moments she got to spend there, were relished, knowing full well that this was a privilege. If the owners of the house were home, she would never be able to enjoy so much time in all the various rooms.

Jeremiah occupied her thoughts, and he had joined her night-time worry list. For some reason, she had not told Harriet about their encounter, who was still relentless in pushing Sybil towards Walt. Her motive was puzzling, but she settled on the fact that they did dance beautifully together, and Harriet seemed obsessed with creating the perfect party.

"Ward is sorting the food. She really is a hard worker since the staff were scaled back, come into her own really. To think she never even used to work in the kitchen!" Harriet threw back her head and laughed. "Anyway, it's all planned out, I thought some mixed canapes would be suffice. And we have enough alcohol to sink a ship. Pardon the pun, war and all. Do take what we don't manage today home, for your dear aunt." Harriet pointed to the fruit cake left on the cake stand. Sybil nodded obediently, with narrowed eyes. She was baffling.

WHEN WAR CAME TO LAUNDRY COTTAGE by Sarah Colliver

Harriet rang the servant's bell beside the fireplace.

"How many do you think you have coming, and are they *all* men?"

Harriet's blonde curls danced on her head as she laughed. "No, not *all* men silly. There's you and me."

Sybil choked on her cake.

"Good God woman, steady. I am joking, we want the troops to have a good time, and you and I can't keep them *all* happy. I know a few land girls and they love to get dolled up when they can. I'm so glad Walter is coming after all because you really do look divine together." Ward appeared in the doorway. "Ward, be a darling and wrap up the rest of this cake for Sybbie to take away. Oh, and some more tea for the pot please."

Harriet increasingly sounded more like the 'lady of the house,' than the nanny. Yet Ward did as she was told and never once seemed perturbed. It was a strange situation. "Any news of when Mrs Bentley is returning?"

WHEN WAR CAME TO LAUNDRY COTTAGE by Sarah Colliver

"Nope. But Daddy called last week, and he heard that she is expected to stay in Devon for the duration. They are happy to have me stay on, as it means someone is keeping the servants in line and can contact them with any issues. It really is the best possible scenario you know, a nanny who doesn't have to nanny! Now sup up, and then let's go upstairs so I can show you which dress I think you should wear."

Sybil had not yet plucked up the courage to tell Aunty Vi that she didn't need the dress after all. She had been so proud of it and ironed it lovingly. Perhaps she could pretend that she wore it, and hope that it didn't get back to her somehow. It would save her feelings and she really did love it. Aunty Vi dabbed at her eyes when Sybil tried it on. "It could have been made for you," she had said. "Worth every one of those potatoes, to see you dressed so pretty."

Harriet opened her bedroom door. The scent of lilies was overpowering. "Where did all these come from?" Sybil gasped as she counted ten vases full of blooms.

"Oh, no one you know." Harriet winked. "Now, over here." She led Sybil to a huge wardrobe and pulled open the door. "So, as you can see, it really is no problem to share a few dresses, I probably won't even wear half of these, darling." She rifled through the rail and settled on a pink satin gown, with diamante detailing.

Sybil had never seen anything so beautiful, except on film stars and never in real life.

"I'm so glad you like it, because this is the one I've chosen for you."

Sybil shook her head. "I couldn't."

"I insist, now over there and off with that old thing, that's it, pop this on. I can help with the buttons at the back."

Sybil's hands trembled as she undressed and slipped the silky material over her head, and watched it cascade along her curves and settle.

"I've got gloves too, but I am not sure we will bother with them, maybe too formal. We want the boys to be enchanted by us, not scared. Oh yes, I simply knew this would look better on you than me. Oh, you could pass as a real society lady. Almost."

Sybil winced at her comment. Jeremiah made her feel like a real lady, in their one meeting, with no more than a handful of sentences exchanged. Whereas Harriet had confirmed exactly what she thought about Sybil, without realising what the words she spoke gave away. She did not see her as an equal at all. Suddenly, Sybil wanted to rip the dress from her skin. It was suffocating. She didn't need to pretend to be anything. This dress, as beautiful as it was, did not belong on her.

"I'm a bit hot. Please can you help me take this off?"

"Darling, you're all flushed! Must be that tea and cake! Here let me pull it over your head. There. Now sit down for a moment."

Sybil re-dressed in her own clothes and sat on the edge of the bed, whilst Harriet carefully rehung the gown in the wardrobe.

"Shall I get the driver to take you home, save your poor feet?" Harriet almost sounded concerned.

"I think a little fresh air would do me good to be honest. Sorry to be a party pooper."

"Not at all, we must have you in fine fettle for our big do, and that handsome GI, who will be desperate to take you in his arms and foxtrot you around our party!"

Sybil felt weary. Harriet was relentless. "It's not *our* party it's yours."

"Well, officially mine, but I want you to experience a large function such as this too, so let's say it's ours, please?"

Sybil knew that arguing was pointless, so she hugged her and headed down the staircase, leaving Harriet to fuss with the wardrobe of dresses. She didn't turn back as she made her way up the drive, but she knew Harriet would be watching from the window.

WHEN WAR CAME TO LAUNDRY COTTAGE by Sarah Colliver

SEVEN

Sybil awoke with a start and sprung out of bed to the window. Her heart raced, and memories of bombing raids and midnight sprints to the Anderson shelter, buried in the garden, clouded her sleepy vision. She pulled back the floral curtain and peered out into the lane, it was empty. She scanned the sky, but all was calm. Creeping along the tiny landing, she paused outside Aunty Vi's room. The door was open enough to peer in and establish that she was sound asleep, so the noise which woke her remained a mystery. She rubbed her eyes and decided it must have been a dream.

Her bladder niggled, and she pulled out the porcelain chamber pot, from beneath her bed, thankful that she no longer needed to scramble out to the privy. The floorboards were dusty and cold underfoot, but her room was cosy. A floral quilt adorned her bed, made by her great- grandmother, Aunty Vi had said. Sybil felt secure beneath the weighty quilt, content in the knowledge that the hands of her own ancestor created it. Various cross-stitched sentiments, framed and hung on the walls, reminded her to 'behave', 'appreciate' and 'be kind'. Sybil shivered and climbed back into bed.

Thoughts jumped around her head, and sleep would be impossible. She was safe, warm, and comfortable, but Mum and Dad would be either working or sat in the air raid shelter shivering. Wondering if their home would still be standing by morning. Tears sprung to her eyes as guilt swamped her. How could she have abandoned them this way? Escape to the safety of the countryside, like an evacuee, sent away from the bombs and danger. Her mind played the sounds of air raids, and with each thunderous explosion, she flinched, and her hands flung to her ears. Tears soaked her nighty and showed no signs of subsiding. Perhaps she should go home. She already knew the answer, her parents would be angry, and send her away again. She wiped her face with her sleeve and fought to regain control of her fast breathing.

She squeezed her eyes shut and Jeremiah appeared. His warm smile beamed at her, as they slowly kissed beneath the moonlit sky. Happiness and calm enveloped her for a moment. Warmth crept through her veins as her body yearned for his touch. Suddenly he was ripped from her arms, and surrounded by a uniformed enemy, who began to beat and kick at him until he lay lifeless. She screamed and threw herself into the corner of the room, where she curled up into a ball and wept. "It was only a dream," she said over and over, until her tears subsided, and she allowed herself to crawl wearily back into bed again.

Sybil winced as the cold, fresh water splashed over her body. Both bracing and unbearable, after a broken night's sleep, it had the immediate effect of waking her brain. The vivid dream about Jeremiah, urged her to find him, check in on him. She needed to know he was alright, even if his feelings did not echo her own. And he had promised her a walk, one day. She so wished he were coming with her to the party. In a funny way, he had helped make up her mind, to attend the party, under her own terms. She would wear her own dress, and she would only dance with whom she chose. She was not, after all, a performing monkey, and Harriet had made it clear that she did not see her as an equal. Sybil was now wondering, what her interest in her was, after all.

In the beginning, Harriet implied that she needed Sybil's help to organise the party, but the truth was that she had planned it herself, her own way, and with no input from Sybil.

"There's a cuppa in the pot, wet and warm, to put a spring in your step!" Aunty Vi's cheery voice carried up the stairs. She pulled on her jumper, darned socks, and headed down the creaky steps. "Freshly poured, here now, sit with me. The village is all a chatter about this party you know. I'm not sure I'm so happy about it, mainly soldiers and land girls they reckon, and we all know how that will end." She buttered a slice of freshly cut bread and passed it across the table. "If your father knew..."

"Come on Aunty, you know as well as I do, everything's changed, the world is topsy turvy. I simply want to have fun, but not the kind of fun you are worried about. I know some of them are only after one thing, but they won't be getting it from me."

WHEN WAR CAME TO LAUNDRY COTTAGE by Sarah Colliver

"Hmm. Well, it isn't always as easy as that my girl. Sometimes, you don't get much choice in these things, so you stay where everyone can see you, and don't be getting too much drink in you. Now, you eat up."

Sybil stood tall, confident in her new-old dress. Aunty Vi helped with her hair, and they pinned it up in the latest victory roll curls. They giggled as she struggled to draw the line down the back of her legs, to simulate stockings. She imagined the look of disgust which would appear on Harriet's face. She must not buckle under her coercive ways. She knew that Harriet would try and talk her into changing into the pink satin dress. But if she wanted to be her friend, she must accept who she is, stop trying to change her.

"You're a sight for sore eyes in that green. Well, if I hadn't known it was Doris's dress, I would say it was made for you." Aunty vi wiped her eyes with her hanky. "You got everything?"

Sybil nodded and picked up the envelope from the table. The gift conundrum remained until five minutes before she left, when she took a piece of writing paper and an envelope from her suitcase, and carefully wrote:

Wishing you the happiest of birthdays, my dear friend Harriet. Please keep this safe, and when you need a favour from me, this is my promise to you.

With love, Sybbie xxx

Excitement grew as she began her walk to Deanwood house, but after five minutes, the car from the big house came hurrying towards her. It stopped only inches away and the driver jumped out and opened the back door.

"Miss Harriet sent me, worried about you being late. Please get in."

Sybil sighed, but was secretly grateful for the ride, if not the controlling sentiment. She was already failing her new promise to stick to her guns. "Thank you, sorry what's your name?"

"No problem, Miss. You can call me Grant."

WHEN WAR CAME TO LAUNDRY COTTAGE by Sarah Colliver

"Thank you, Grant. You've saved my legs for the dancing tonight."

"Yes miss."

Before the turning of the long driveway up to Deanwood House, a familiar uniformed figure, strolled along the path to the village.

"Please Grant, stop the car! Let me out, and then do continue, and let Harriet know I am on my way. Thank you."

Sybil hopped out and slammed the door shut. "Jeremiah!"

The soldier turned and smiled. "Miss Sybil."

"No, just Sybil, we've been through this. I'm so happy to see you." Relief that he was here, unscathed, beautiful, and looking deep into her eyes. What was this connection? No-one had ever got under her skin this way, and it was hard to describe how he made her feel. It was like when you go away, and long for home, he was home.

He gestured to his two companions, to continue without him. They raised their eyebrows and turned to head on to the village.

He took her hands in his and admired her from top to toe, shaking his head, drinking her in. "You are a picture."

Hope flooded her. "I'm on my way to that party I told you about."

"I think the whole of the county has heard about that party." His smooth voice was music to her ears.

"So, you'll come?"

He shook his head, puzzled. "You must know, that isn't possible?"

"You are my guest. I am allowed to invite whoever I wish!"

"I don't think that extends to me."

"What if I say, that unless you come with me, I won't go either?"

WHEN WAR CAME TO LAUNDRY COTTAGE by Sarah Colliver

"That is flattering, I can't lie. But we both know that isn't true. You must go, you cannot let your friend down, and you are way too pretty to waste." He lifted her hand to his mouth and kissed it.

Grant pulled back out of the drive, and stopped beside them, this time the door flung open, and Harriet propelled herself out. "Sybbie, darling, is he bothering you?" Her mouth curled the words out in disgust.

"Harriet! Please don't be rude to my friend. Jeremiah this is Harriet, Harriet this is Jeremiah."

She reluctantly held her hand out in greeting, shook his hand briefly and then wiped her hand on the back of her dress. "Come on now Sybbie, we must go, Walter is already there, and the band has begun playing. You need to change too."

"Well, firstly, I'm not changing, I am ready and happy with how I'm dressed. Secondly, I want Jeremiah to come and be my guest. In fact, I am not coming, unless he does." Sybil took his hand and squeezed it.

Jeremiah blushed. "This isn't necessary, please go with Miss Harriet and have a great time."

Sybil stood firm. "Well?"

Harriet's stone face erupted into laughter. "Well of course, you simply must come too. Why not? Where did you say you were based?"

Sybil pulled Jeremiah towards the car, before Harriet could change her mind.

"No, really, this isn't a good idea." Jeremiah's voice, full of concern, did not prevent Sybil from continuing.

"He is based over the fields from my cottage, aren't you? Please get in the car, don't say no."

He paused for a moment, glancing at Grant, who continued to stare straight ahead and make no sound.

"Well okay then, but for five minutes, then I'm gone."

Sybil hugged Harriet. "Thank you, thank you! I knew you wouldn't let us down."

She smiled back. "You still have enough time to change too."

Sybil wondered if she could fight the obligation she now felt to Harriet, but squeezed Jeremiah's hand

WHEN WAR CAME TO LAUNDRY COTTAGE by Sarah Colliver

tight, awash with excitement for how their evening would unfold.

Grant came around to open the door for them, and Jeremiah exited from the opposite side. He straightened up and puffed out, adjusting his cap, before coming around to join them. Harriet flounced in through the door, greeting her guests and directing them to the champagne and canapes. She was in her element.

"Come on, let's have a drink and then we can dance." Sybil swiped two glasses from the tray and handed one to him. "Follow me." The band was deafening, and the floor packed like sardines. "Look, there's Walt!"

Walt stood abreast of the ornate fireplace, but his face paled as they neared him. "Walt, this is Jeremiah."

Jeremiah stood upright and saluted Walt.

"At ease soldier." Walt pulled Sybil in close, and whispered, "What the hell are you doing? Do you know the danger you have put him in? I have nothing against 'them' as such, but there are plenty in this room who do. The best thing you can do is slip away quietly with him, away from here."

Jeremiah's reluctance suddenly made sense. She grabbed his firm arm tight and turned to scan the now hushed room. They were a spectacle, a circus act to be gawped at. Never had Sybil felt so stupid, so naïve. Concerned for him, she sought his eyes to offer reassurance, but he stared at the ground.

Harriet entered the room and with ease addressed her guests. "This is supposed to be a party. My birthday party! Who told the band to stop playing? You are all happy to come and drink my champagne, eat my canapes, so you can damn well behave too. This man is my guest, and you should all do well to remember that, or you are welcome to leave..."

A shuffle of GIs headed out, muttering obscenities and then Harriet was over by the band, who struck up 'Happy birthday,' despite losing one of their singers to the disapproving exodus. The crowds hush evolved into chatter and laughter, as they began to sing along to the band. Harriet commanded the scene as she beamed and bowed to the guests, thanking them for the sentiment. She was born to manipulate crowds. She had aged, from the youthful nanny on the bus, to a powerful woman, used to hosting large events. What a complex puzzle she was.

The moment of threat passed but Sybil's knees still quivered. She refused to let go of Jeremiah's arm.

Walt stepped close to Jeremiah. "I think you should take this woman onto the dance floor, I know for a fact she's a mover, so you better live up to it." He smiled. "What are you waiting for, that's an order soldier."

Sybil kissed Walt on the cheek. "Thank you."

He shook his head and seemed to have so much more to say, but instead gently pushed them onto the dance floor, where the music swept them away.

When she and Walt had danced, it felt as though they were dance partners, the chemistry was in the movements and fluidity, as it would be with a professional. But now, with Jeremiah holding her close, they clung to each other, as though they may suffocate if separated. Sybil felt he was part of her, a missing piece which she didn't know was lost, until that moment. 'A nightingale sang in Berkley Square' played, it seemed, for them alone, and with their bodies pressed together they barely moved, lost in each other. The depth of connection was intense and wonderful, yet terrifying and overwhelming. She was unsure if she would laugh or cry, but she never wanted to let him go.

The evening passed quickly, as though she barely had a moment to breathe. Each moment precious, and Sybil knew she would carry this night around forever. He offered to walk her home, but she explained that she would be staying over. By the end of the evening, bodies littered the house, either too drunk to walk, or too 'involved' to care.

They took a drink out into the night sky, leaving a frantic Ward, trying to adhere to the blackout rules around the guests and endless rooms. It was quiet, and neither felt the need to fill the space with words. An ease sat between them, being present together, was enough.

Sybil remembered the maze. "Follow me, let's have an adventure together."

Jeremiah took Sybil's hand and she led him away from the house, and into the mysterious hedge puzzle. "I've never been in one of these before, so you better take care of me."

Jeremiah pulled her close. "I would do anything for you, my Sybil."

Sybil leaned up toward him on tiptoe and kissed his lips. Her body tingled, at his touch.

"Come on let's go in a bit further." He pulled her in deeper. Exhilarated and giddy, it was as though the world beyond no longer existed. On reaching the middle, a stone seat sat outside a locked shed. They slumped on the seat and finished their glasses, dropping them to the floor.

Sybil took his face in her hands and kissed him again. She never knew it was possible to be so consumed with what she supposed was desire. The few occasions when Philip had kissed her, she felt nothing, but Jeremiah awoke something within her, something she never wanted to let go of.

"Do you feel this too?" she whispered.

He nodded, his eyes penetrating her soul. "But this cannot exist outside of this maze, you do know that?"

"Don't say that. Why would you say that?"

"Stop it. You KNOW why. You saw what happened when we arrived."

Tears sprung to her eyes. "So, we must do what other people want? Even if it is the wrong thing?"

Jeremiah wiped the tears from her cheeks with his hands. "People don't just throw their words, Sybil. Words can be cutting enough, sure, but terrible things happen. Do you know that us here, me sitting next to you, is enough to bring down a whole heap of trouble, but to kiss you like this, well..." He grazed his lips across hers. "If you had seen what my eyes have...the horrors, the torture." He lowered his gaze to the floor. She knew what he was doing, he was trying to force dreadful memories away from his mind. "I'm glad you

WHEN WAR CAME TO LAUNDRY COTTAGE by Sarah Colliver

haven't seen these things because you cannot be haunted by things you never saw."

"We all have things up here, that we carry, that haunt us." Sybil tapped her head.

He knelt in front of her lap, gripped her hands, and locked eyes with her. "Do you know what it means to be seen? I mean *really* seen. Seen for who I am, as a man, as Jeremiah Thomas, soldier, sure. But I am also a carpenter, who loves to sing, who is slowly losing his belief in God with every new injustice and act of violence. Jeremiah, who wants to choose who he can marry, who will have his children, where he lives and on what street he can walk." His brown eyes threatened tears. "Where I live, freedom isn't on offer for us. Signs and instructions are put up everywhere, to remind us of the rules, keep us in our place. We can come over here and fight a war against oppression, tyranny. But we aren't even allowed to do that alongside the white men." He paused, swallowed back his rising anger.

He sighed and then inhaled a long breath. "And then there's you, Miss Sybil." With such softness, he peppered kisses across her face. "And you see beyond the colour of my skin, it isn't even a thing with you, you're blind to it. I've never known this in my whole life before. With you, I almost believe this could happen. I can hang on to that. You, will stay in here with me, always." He moved her hand up to his chest and held it there, while he kissed her again. Sybil wanted him to sweep her away, to a place where only love existed. No war, no prejudice. Just them.

"When we have our children, we can teach them to treat people for who they are, not what they look like." Sybil smiled, hoping they would have his dark, dreamy eyes. It was as though she could foresee their entwined destiny, and although it seemed impossible, it was also inevitable.

"This moment together, now, this is all we have. All we can ever have."

Sybil would not give up that easily, the depths of her feelings threatened to suffocate her, at the thought of not being with him. She would figure it out. "Wasn't it wonderful though? Dancing together all evening.

WHEN WAR CAME TO LAUNDRY COTTAGE by Sarah Colliver

Being in your arms. You and I are *meant* to be. You can't change that."

Jeremiah drew her in tight, and she could feel his heart beating. This was where she belonged, there could never be another. She was limited in experience with men, but it was true what the love stories say, you know when it happens. His strong hand gently rubbed her back.

"Does she always instruct you? Miss Harriet? She told you to change, in the car."

Sybil thought for a moment. "That's an interesting way of putting it. I would say… she is bossy and knows her own mind, but instruct? No, I don't think so."

He stood and lifted her up off the ground until their faces were level. "I'm glad you didn't change, because when I close my eyes, I will see you tonight, in this green dress, with your curls and those lips. You, my Sybil, were the belle of the ball. This is how you will always be to me."

Sybil blushed but believed every word he spoke. To him, she was beautiful. "And you, my handsome prince charming. Always. You already occupy my thoughts and my dreams... please be careful. I need you." She kissed him gently, but conjured all her love, devotion, and affection into it, she hoped he would feel the power.

"You know, I have to go now."

"Stay with me. Please, if like you say, we only have now, stay. I have my own room here tonight."

His eyes, full of desire, closed as he kissed her slower, deeply. She felt his body respond against her hip, and hoped he would carry her upstairs and answer the call of her yearning body.

"If you only knew how much I want to. But I can't, I'm leaving, because I care so much for you. It would only complicate this more, make it worse."

He carried her back through the maze, and she clung to him, not wanting to ever let him go. Silent tears streamed down her face. She forced her brain to repeat the words, 'this is not over.'

WHEN WAR CAME TO LAUNDRY COTTAGE by Sarah Colliver

At the entrance to the maze, he placed her down, and they walked around to the front of the house hand in hand. He looked around, the space now devoid of people, and kissed her again. He pulled back, and as though he were sketching her image in his mind, drank in every detail. "Goodbye, my beautiful Sybil."

He turned and ran, away from the house, from her, up the long driveway. Sybil watched him disappear, swallowing the lump in her throat, questioning the overpowering emotions she felt about him. How could she feel so strong towards him, when they had spent only a few hours together? You could blame the war, and the urgency it provoked, the need and craving of a release from worry and fear. But she already knew it was more than that. In her heart, they were destined to be together, and the war brought him from the other side of the world, just for their paths to cross. It was as though one shared word between them, equated to a hundred in normal conversation. As though they already knew one another.

Suddenly weary, she dragged herself up the grand staircase, and knocked quietly on Harriet's bedroom door, there was no answer, and rather than knock again she crept inside. A dim table lamp was on in the far corner and cast shadows from the bed onto the wall. She stifled a gasp and tip-toed forward to see who it was. A uniform lay strewn across the floor, discarded next to Harriet's dress. The snoring bed companion was Walt, and crouched on the floor next to the bed was Harriet, who, now alerted to her watcher, turned, and scowled. Sybil ran to leave, closely followed by Harriet, who quietly closed the door behind them and ushered her along the corridor, into her room.

"What are you doing creeping about?" Harriet pulled open a wardrobe and slipped on a dressing gown, to cover her nakedness. "Why is your face covered in makeup, have you been crying?"

"You slept with Walt?"

"Oh, grow up. I told you, they all want the same thing. I took one for the team, it could have been you."

"What were you doing on the floor?"

"I dropped something. Where's lover boy?"

WHEN WAR CAME TO LAUNDRY COTTAGE by Sarah Colliver

"He left. He says we can't be together."

"He has a point darling. You hardly 'blend in' together. But he could have stayed, what difference would one night make after the entrance you two made tonight? I dread to think what will happen to him now."

"Huh?"

"You cannot be that naïve? No one is that wet behind the ears. Stop crying. There's nothing you can do about it now. He will have to fend for himself."

Reality hit Sybil, her blinkered affection for him, had endangered him. What had she done? Her body trembled.

"You do have it bad, don't you? I must say, you could have given me a little warning about him darling. I absolutely hate being put into positions like that. It's a good job I can think on my feet, or Lord knows what chaos would have ensued. God only knows what the Bentley's will think, once the staff tell them we had 'one' in their house as a guest. Now, sit down on the bed and I shall grab us both a brandy. I will say though, if I were into that kind of thing, which I'm not by the way, he would be the sort of one I would go for, something about him."

Sybil threw herself onto her knees and prayed, prayed for Jeremiah to be safe. She would agree to let him go if he were safe. Her white knuckles squeezed tight as she repeated over and over her pledge to God, and hoped that He would hear her, despite the proclamation Jeremiah had made about doubting His existence.

EIGHT

"Oh, you've really done it now." Aunty Vi opened the front door. She must have been watching from the window for her. "I expected you back this morning young lady. It's almost teatime! What would your father say?"

Sybil trudged nearer to her aunt, in no mood for a ticking off. "Nothing to tell him. If you are referring to Jeremiah, then there really is nothing to tell. Because we cannot be together. Because people are cruel, ignorant, and vile. Do you know that he is more of a gentleman than any other man I have ever met. He is a carpenter, and he's kind, and he loves to sing. Aunty, to me he is everything."

Aunty Vi's face crumpled on seeing Sybil so broken. "Come on inside, I've boiled up some water in the copper and you can have a nice soak in front of the fire. We have a box of bath salts in the cupboard. Let's get yesterday's make up off your face and give that hair a brush."

"Who tells you all these things anyway? How does the word get around so quickly? Do you think these gossips will know if he is ok, because…" her mouth felt dry, and she sipped on a cold tea. "Because Harriet thinks I've put him in danger now. Thing is, I love him and the thought of him being hurt in anyway, feels as though it's killing me. I can't breathe!"

"Now, now. Shush, come on out of those clothes and into the tub. It's nice and soothing." She helped her into the water and stoked the fire. "We can listen out for news on him. If that helps. But I'm afraid she may be right. They don't take well to his sort mixing with whites."

"His sort? He's just a man. A decent man. The man I will marry. That's all."

Aunty Vi put up her hands. "I didn't mean it like that, trying to explain how it is, is all. I have nothing against him. All I care about is if he treats you well. If he does, then he is welcome in my home, if he doesn't, I don't care who he be, where he came from or what his colour, he isn't coming near."

That sentence gave a tiny grain of hope, because Jeremiah was decent, polite, and charming, and if that was all the mattered, truly, to Aunty Vi, then at least in her home they stood a chance. Aunty Vi took an old comb from the shelf and began to pull out the remaining pins from her, now messy, hair. It was soothing, and Sybil finally felt a little calmer.

"Do you promise to tell me as soon as you hear anything? I may be able to get Walt to find out, he was decent to him. I must know though, its driving me insane." She was rambling on and her exhausted words barely comprehensible.

The rhythmic brushing of her hair, and the warmth of the fire, pulled closed her eyes and she realised how exhausted she felt. Never had she been more grateful to climb into her own bed.

She slept through dawn, breakfast, and at ten Aunty Vi sat at the foot of Sybil's bed, and gently rubbed her feet. "Wake up my love. I brought you a cup of tea."

Sybil blinked away her sleep and stretched out her arms. Her mind still sleepy and slow. "Thank you. What time is it?"

"Ten."

"Oh, I'm so sorry. I should be up." She never wanted another sip of alcohol; her head pounded.

"Drink this first, you've had a long couple of days. It seems to have taken a toll on you."

Sybil slurped the warm tea, grateful to be so well cared for. It was then, that moment when her brain caught up with her waking body and her face dropped. "Jeremiah? Have you heard anything? Oh, what have I done?"

Aunty Vi took the teacup from her shaking hand and placed it onto the windowsill. "Come on, there, there." She squashed next to her on the bed, and pulled her into her soft, ample bosom. "I promise if I hear anything I will let you know, but this doesn't help anyone." She took a hanky from her pinny and handed it to Sybil. "Wipe those tears. We have much to get on with. I know you're upset and worried, but that doesn't change the facts."

Aunty Vi slid off the bed and paused in the doorway. "You know, I'm not sure this Harriet is someone you should be spending time with. There's been lots of questions raised about her. How can a 'nanny' behave the way she does when her mistress is away? It doesn't make sense to me, nor anyone else it seems. And another thing, what does she want with you?" She scratched her head and closed the door behind her.

WHEN WAR CAME TO LAUNDRY COTTAGE by Sarah Colliver

Sybil's initial flood in defence of her friend, (after all she made it possible for Jeremiah to stay at the party) was replaced with questions of her own, and no matter how hard she tried, she came up with no answers. It was a puzzle and made no sense. But overwhelming guilt pecked at her, and she climbed out of bed to get dressed. Aunty Vi was right, she couldn't wither away in bed, when there was so much to do, no matter how much her heart ached, and gut churned.

NINE

"They're here! Finish up, don't keep them waiting." Aunty Vi was still enamoured by those from the 'big house'.

Sybil threw off her pinny and her arms around Aunty Vi, planting a firm kiss on her cheek. "You sure it's ok? I know you had a list for me to do."

Aunty Vi playfully smacked her bottom. "That list will be waiting for you later, now get yourself away girl, before I change my mind. Have fun, but remember what I said, be a bit, well on your guard. I don't trust her…"

Sybil retied her head scarf, and marched out onto the lane, where Harriet sat waiting in the car. "I thought we were going for a walk? Hello Grant."

"Miss Sybil." He nodded.

Harriet raised her expertly painted eyebrows. "Drive on then. We are, but we must get to the walk first, silly. I have a tot of brandy for when we get there too. Cigarette?" Harriet opened an ornately engraved silver cigarette case, fully stocked, and adorned with her initials.

"No thanks."

After a few minutes, Sybil realised they were heading close to Jeremiah's camp and her stomach lurched. Was Harriet scheming?

"I know what you're thinking darling, why are we heading out in this direction? Well, the simple answer is, because I want to! There are beautiful views over

WHEN WAR CAME TO LAUNDRY COTTAGE by Sarah Colliver

this way, and I have dug out my camera and thought we could take some photographs."

Sybil's heart sank a little, it hadn't even occurred to Harriet that Jeremiah was based this way.

"Why the frown Sybbie? I thought you would enjoy a walk and a chat."

"Do you think we would be walking anywhere near the camp?"

"Ah, the penny drops, is your exotic fellow there then? Yes, now you come to mention it I vaguely recall you saying something about it. I'm sure we could kill two birds with one stone. If that would remove the awful frown from your face, you know it's really not good for your skin; frowning."

For the first time in a week, hope sparked within at the possibility of seeing his beautiful face again, no matter how much of a long shot it was. A grin crept across her face, and she willed the car to speed up.

"Stop here please. We should be a couple of hours, so you can go and come back or stay here." Harriet checked her bag and waited for Grant to open the door. "Off we go then. This way." She linked arms with Sybil and together they strode enthusiastically towards a stile leading on to a field. It was marvellous to be enjoying such freedoms, and hard not to let the clouds of war and suffering dampen the experience.

Leaving behind the wide-open fields, they ambled on through a thicket, where engines and muffled voices echoed. Harriet put her finger to her lips and Sybil erupted into nervous giggles. They were not doing anything wrong, but her breaths quickened. It was the back of the camp, and the perimeter protected by barbed wire. "Best not get any closer."

Harriet tutted. "Really you are a frightful coward. I thought you wanted to find out about your man. Let's go around the side, I just saw one of 'them'. You could ask him if he knows him?" She pushed her forwards, and Sybil staggered near the fence, alerting the soldier to her presence. He wiped his hands on his apron and took two steps towards her.

"You shouldn't be here. Go."

WHEN WAR CAME TO LAUNDRY COTTAGE by Sarah Colliver

"Please, do you know Jeremiah Thomas? He's based here. I must know if he's ok."

"I don't know what you think you are doing Ma'am, but you need to leave. They'll arrest you if you're caught here, and me, well I'm not even supposed to talk to you. Go." He turned his back and headed back into the kitchen.

Sybil spun only to realise she was alone, and Harriet nowhere to be seen. Her dampened spirits shortened her patience, as she stomped away in fury. If she were to enquire at the camp barrier, to any white soldier, she would only endanger him further. She was stuck.

Back through the trees into the open field, Sybil perched on the stump of an old oak, and scanned the horizon for Harriet. Perhaps Walt would be able to dig around. He was sympathetic to them at the party, and Harriet had obviously gone beyond the friendship stakes with him. She pushed her finger into a hole in her stockings. They had been darned multiple times and there was more darning than stocking left. Her shoes were now filthy and would need a polish before Aunty Vi caught sight of them.

"Darling, there you are. I couldn't find you! Sneaked off to relieve myself and you were gone. Any joy?"

Sybil shook her head.

"Smoke? Brandy? Looks like you could do with it."

"Yes, to both." Sybil slid out a cigarette each and Harriet lit them both. They took it in turns to sip the brandy, which burned her throat. She still did not enjoy it one bit. "I had an idea."

"Oh?"

"I cannot endanger his life any more than I stupidly have, by asking around after him. But you, you could find out from Walt…if he's heard anything at all. He would know. If anyone does."

Harriet drew smoke deep into her lungs and laid back on the grass.

"Well? It really is the only way I can think of. Even Aunty Vi has not heard anything, and she usually knows everything before it even happens."

WHEN WAR CAME TO LAUNDRY COTTAGE by Sarah Colliver

"I'm not promising. If, If I see Walter again, and it becomes appropriate to drop it into conversation, then I shall. Right?"

Sybil nodded. She had no other plan. It would have to do. "Did you want to take some photographs? Shall we find a nice spot?"

"No, turns out my film was full, must buy some more. Come on, let's head back up the hill darling."

As the car drew up outside Laundry Cottage, a sinking feeling drained the colour from Sybil's face. Something was wrong. She couldn't verbalise this, although her paled complexion indicated all was not well.

"Sybbie? What is it? You suddenly look dreadful. Shall I get Grant to help you inside?"

"No," she said and kissed Harriet on the cheek, sprung out of the car and through the gate in a flash. "Aunty Vi?" She called out in fear, hoping nothing had happened to her. And then her thoughts swung to her parents, and their precarious situation in the city. Maybe it was them. Whatever was happening, she felt it through her entire body. "Aunty Vi? Where are you?" With the house empty, she sprinted outside and up to the very end where the brook skimmed their garden. "Aunty Vi! What's happened?"

A sudden awareness of her aunt's elderly frame, or was it that she had simply aged a lifetime since the morning? It was obvious that unwelcome news was afoot. A crumpled-up brown envelope fell to the ground, and she stared through Sybil.

"He's gone. My boy. My darling boy."

Sybil scooped up the telegram: the thing dreaded by every wife and mother, the knock at the door with that sinister brown envelope, but today it was the turn of Laundry Cottage. A day Aunty Vi had always feared. Sybil read and re-read the words: KILLED IN ACTION.

She instinctively pulled her devastated aunty into a firm embrace, and her shock instantly switched to racking sobs. Sybil led her up the garden to the house

WHEN WAR CAME TO LAUNDRY COTTAGE by Sarah Colliver

and sat her down in a chair, next to the range. "I'm going to make some tea. We need a strong cup, so I'm getting the fresh stuff out, not yesterdays." But Aunty Vi was too far gone to acknowledge the conversation and stared at the framed picture of her uniformed boy on the mantel piece, smart and proud.

Sybil moved about the kitchen, unsure what words she could offer. "I'm so sorry. It must be such a shock for you."

Aunty Vi took the steaming tea from Sybil and nodded. "It's the one thing I have feared this whole war. Had a telegram in the last war, you see, your Uncle Cyril. He fell, in a faraway place. The war to end all wars they said." She wiped her nose with her hanky. "The Somme is where he lays, and for what? Not so that our poor, poor boy, Robert, could end his life in another battle. I know that much." She reached up and took hold of the photograph. "That smile of his, could never stay mad at him for long. Little bugger he was when he was a young 'un. But win you round with a flash of those blue eyes and that smile."

WHEN WAR CAME TO LAUNDRY COTTAGE by Sarah Colliver

Sybil drew a chair close, and together they sat, mostly in silence, but with an occasional sniff or memory. She wondered how Aunty Vi would cope, but felt comfort to know, she could take care of her at such a devastating time.

"I'm alone now. My Cyril, my Robert, gone, gone to be with my little girls." She wiped her nose again. Aunty Vi's two daughters died in infancy, and she cherished the photograph of each of them she had.

"Can you pass me a fresh hanky, from the drawer over there, and bring the photographs of my girls too. I want them all next to me."

Sybil pulled open the drawer, it smelt of dried lavender, and gathered the frames from the shelf. "Here Aunty." She kissed her on the cheek and carefully placed the photographs next to her cousin Robert, who stood proud in his uniform, staring back at them. Her own little family gathered upon her kitchen table. "Shall we light a candle for them all?"

Aunty Vi nodded amid the fresh tears now flowing. "Yes. Just the one, for them all."

WHEN WAR CAME TO LAUNDRY COTTAGE by Sarah Colliver

The days that followed, brought a flood of neighbours with flowers, baked offerings and simple words of condolence. It evidenced the tight community, and emphasised that it was not all about gossip, but there was deep-rooted affection for each other. It was heart-warming, and although nothing could make the situation better, knowing that others cared, or unfortunately had been through the same, did help with the sting.

TEN

The pull to find Jeremiah was overwhelming. The GI days off were staggered, depending on the colour of their skin. This statement was incomprehensible to Sybil. She was always taught, that whatever was on the inside; good intentions, compassion, kindness, was what mattered. Her mum's brother, Uncle Frank, came back from the Great War, broken in spirit and body. They looked after him, nurtured him back to health, but his visible wounds caused heads to turn. Gasps and mutterings as they passed him. Her family learned that people's shells did not change whether a person was kind, bad, or worthy of love.

Today was when the black GIs got to shop and drink in the village. The landlord in the pub, initially fought the segregation brought over by the Americans, but the threats of boycotting and the need to feed his large family, since the death of his son, overrode his own beliefs. It was said, that he welcomed them in and made sure they felt at ease in his pub, when possible.

Armed with a shopping list and empty bags, she intended to mill about the village, hoping to 'bump into' Jeremiah. She approached the bench near the post box and perched, steadying her nerves, what if the news was bad? What if something had happened to him? She shook the negative thoughts from her head, and a familiar figure caught her eye. Harriet was climbing out of the car, and heading between the church and Memorial Hall, close to where they had enjoyed their first picnic together. Her voice failed to sound a 'hello' and she sank back onto the bench. This wasn't about her, and if she engaged it would lead to questions and inevitably end with her abandoning the mission and doing Harriet's bidding. Perhaps she was meeting with someone, the mysterious man who sent the glut of lilies. Or Walt and he might know something about Jeremiah. Five minutes passed, with her racing thoughts debating her next move.

Before her brain could decide what to do, her feet carried her along the little gravel path through the already trodden brambles, and towards the breathtaking view. It felt like years since they first sat together, soaking up the sunshine. She scanned the horizon as Harriet was nowhere to be seen. She couldn't have got too far though. Sybil slumped on the seat, as she continued to eye the area for movement. Far to the right of the field, just visible amongst a small peppering of pine, stood some kind of wooden building. Perhaps she was there? Why? Could she even be bothered to find out? She checked her watch, it was only 9.15am. The village would still be devoid of GIs and so heaving her now weary body, she headed for the trees. The simple scenario that Harriet and Walt may be sharing a stolen kiss, now gone, she berated herself for wasting energy on a false errand.

On approach to the coppice, laughter echoed. It was Harriet. Sybil's brow furrowed, and she suddenly felt as though she were intruding on something. She snuck as close as she could, without being seen, and listened. Groans of pleasure. Was it Walt after all? She craned her neck around the tree. Harriet stood with her dress pulled up around her waist, stockings exposed, and no knickers. Knelt beneath her outstretched legs, an enthusiastic British officer gripped her bottom with his hands, as he burrowed his face up between her thighs.

"Oh, you are such a naughty officer…but you really are… very…good…at this." Harriet's words were broken by whimpers.

Sybil watched in wonder and curiosity. She had never seen anything that personal before, and blushed at the sight of what was happening. Harriet grabbed his head hard, rocking with his movements, as she moaned and her face flushed pink.

Sybil ran, as quietly and as fast as she could, away from the spectacle she had encountered. Conflicting feelings of disgust and yearning flooded her, as she returned to the bench by the post box in the village. She felt exposed, as though everyone knew what she had seen and fought to control her breath and calm her thoughts. No one knows. No one. Who was he? Was she working her way through all the soldiers of the area? She was exactly the type of girl who her parents warned her about. Or was she simply making the most of her time away from home, enjoying the freedom that brought. So many thoughts clouded her mind, and the only clear one, was that the war had changed everything.

She lurked around town for an hour, but after completing the shopping list as best as she could with the shortages, and with not a single soldier appearing, she decided to abort her mission and head home. Perhaps their day off had been cancelled, or they had new orders and left the area. War time was full of uncertainties, all she could do was hope that Jeremiah would one day contact her. She crossed her fingers as she headed up the road to home, hoping to make it before the impending rain arrived.

"Sybil!" Walt's familiar voice called out.

Her face blushed, as the recollection of him snoring in Harriet's bed, popped into her mind. "Hey! How are you?"

"Oh, you know."

"Been dancing anywhere lately? You know your wife is a lucky lady!"

"Huh, taught me everything I know." His face lit up at the thought of her. And Sybil wondered if he felt any guilt about his liaison with Harriet.

Sybil remembered his dark thoughts that first night they met. Everyone, it seemed, carried some sort of darkness around, but especially in war time, where horrific scenes could explode literally anywhere at any time.

"I wanted to catch you, smoke?" Walt offered the pack and Sybil gladly accepted. He drew on his cigarette, before speaking. "I have news, about your friend."

"Jeremiah?" Sybil's face flushed and her heart sped up, until she could hardly speak.

He nodded. "He's in a bad, bad way."

Sybil chewed her nail. Confused, she said, "Has he been injured?"

"Yes. He's in the hospital."

"What happened? We haven't had a raid around here for ages." Her mind sped through thoughts, picking them up and discarding them until she felt dizzy. "Has he been sent away to fight somewhere?"

"Listen, you know I'm not allowed to give you any information about things like that. But what I can say is, that his injuries were nothing to do with the war. I want you to know, that I am ashamed about what happened to him, and I want no part in it."

Sybil rubbed at her forehead, as she fought to digest his words. Her eyes beseeched him to continue.

"He was beaten, by some of my men. Thankfully, I arrived before they finished him off, but he was too savagely beaten to send back to the States. His right arm is crushed, and we think, beyond repair. I have him in a private room at the hospital and have given the staff instructions not to allow visitors, in case they go back and finish off the job they started."

"It's all my fault. How will he earn a living after the war? He's a carpenter you know. Will he survive? I must go to him. Is he safe? What can we do? Walt, what can we do? What is wrong with people? What did he do wrong? Nothing!" Sybil's words expelled into screams.

Walt grabbed Sybil and pulled her close. "Sybil, breathe, just breathe, this isn't going to help."

Sybil's verbal assault dissipated into sobs of despair as he gently rocked her.

"I can get you a pass to visit him. But you must be discreet. And you also must understand that I am one man, one man cannot fight the laws of segregation alone. There is only so much I can do."

"When, when can I see him? Can I take Aunty Vi with me? Please say yes. We could sneak in, Aunty Vi knows everyone, and she will help me. Can I go now? When?"

WHEN WAR CAME TO LAUNDRY COTTAGE by Sarah Colliver

"Stop! Stop this, listen please, I am going to drop off instructions, and you will have to be patient. But you also must accept that this is doomed, you and he, well it's impossible."

Sybil swallowed and began to calm a little. "Walt, how can I thank you?"

He sighed. "I've seen enough pointless deaths in the last two years, I don't want another on my conscience. You two, well, you seemed as though you were made for each other at that party and it reminded me of how much I love my wife. If someone told me I wasn't allowed to be with her, for no good reason, I'm not sure how I would deal with that. Now, I must get back, go home and as soon as I can, I will be in touch. He'll be as safe as I can make it for now."

Sybil ran home, faster than her legs had ever managed before. Her mind replayed the dream she had when they kissed beneath the moonlight until he was ripped from her and beaten by uniformed soldiers. Only she had assumed they were Nazi soldiers, but in fact they were GIs. She flung open the kitchen door and shouted, "Where are you?"

"What is it, what's the matter?" Aunty Vi ran into the kitchen, leaving the boiling copper bubbling behind her.

"He's in hospital!"

"Who?"

"Jeremiah! They beat him, almost killed him."

"Sit yourself down girl and take a breath before you collapse. And then start again."

Sybil slumped into the carver chair, and once her breath calmed, spoke. "Walt found me along the road, and told me that his men set about Jeremiah, and almost killed him. Aunty, it was for dancing with me, for being with me. It's my fault. But he is going to arrange for us, you and me, to sneak in, so we can visit him, let him know we care, because he is all alone, and has no one, and Walt has told the hospital staff not to let anyone else in, in case they find him and kill him!"

Aunty Vi was pouring two brandies from the emergency bottle. "Here, sip this now. You must slow down." She took her brandy to the copper and paced back and forwards sipping. "Well. This is a situation…but he is someone's son. His mother would be broken-hearted about this. The only comfort my Robert dying offers, is that he can't be hurt no more. The thought that with this war killing men left right and centre, isn't enough to stop folk turning on their own side, well, what a state to be in…when are we to visit?"

"Walt said we must be patient, he will sort it and let us know. He has to be careful, as do we, because we could endanger him more. We can't risk that. What if they do kill him? If he dies…"

"STOP THIS RIGHT NOW. This is not going to help your Jeremiah, this fuss. You need a calm head on those shoulders, you must be clear thinking girl. There is no room for these hysterics. If you want to help him, you must get a grip of yourself. Now, I'm thinking, we could borrow a nurse's uniform…blend in…"

Sybil threw herself at Aunty Vi, and hugged her tight, full of gratitude and love, and for her quick thinking. From within this little old lady was emerging a strong, brave, and forward-thinking character, which Sybil felt had her own history of battles to tell. She hoped that one day, Aunty Vi would confide in her and share them, but for now, at least, their focus was Jeremiah.

ELEVEN

She crossed her fingers and mouthed silent prayers, but the formidable figure of Aunty Vi, so short in stature but powered by determination, encouraged her to believe that they could pull this off. It seemed that once Aunty set her mind to something, nothing could sway her. She was sure Robert sat at the bottom of this. That in her mind, she was going to assist a soldier far away from home, someone like her own son. Sybil had not confided in Harriet, in fact the only people who knew about the plan was Aunty Vi, and Walt, and somehow, she knew he would not breathe a word to anyone, including Harriet.

Under cover of the black out, they crossed the road at the front of the hospital where the ambulances pull in and climbed the steps purposefully. As expected, the imposing figure of Sister McMahon greeted them, and led them through a door, where they hung up their coats, thus exposing their volunteer uniforms. "Do as I say and follow me," she ordered as she headed out into the busy corridor. They strode to the end, where a nurses station, a tidy desk and lamp stood, commanding the view of the entire ward. To the left, on a closed door hung the sign: RESTRICTED ACCESS-CONTAGION!

Sister McMahon reclaimed her chair behind the command centre, "Thank you nurse you may resume your rounds." The young nurse scurried away. "You may go in, he can have some water, which is on the stand." She pointed to the restricted access door, and then began to leaf through her paperwork.

Aunty Vi followed close behind Sybil who pushed open the door, her heart pounded so hard she felt she may keel over. The dim room was stifling. Her hands shook as Aunty Vi grabbed them, and nodded, "Deep breaths, you cannot help him if you aren't calm. He needs reassurance."

WHEN WAR CAME TO LAUNDRY COTTAGE by Sarah Colliver

Sybil nodded and fought to regain control of her conflicting emotions, so incredibly grateful for Aunty Vi's presence. She tiptoed to the bed, and gasped.

Jeremiah was unrecognisable. His scabbed face, still puffy and bruised, bore no resemblance to the man she had clung to at Deanwood House. "It's not him. It's not…"

Aunty Vi shouted at her in a stern whisper, "Stop this. The swelling will reduce, you aren't helping him, doing this! You should leave if you can't help this poor man! Pull yourself together girl or get out!"

Aunty Vi perched on the chair and gently took his hand. "You poor, poor thing. What have they done to you? There, it's alright now, we'll look after you."

Sybil cowered in the corner, unable to look upon the man who stole her heart. The pain of his suffering wounded her. He was there, lying in that bed, broken, because of her. Because she was so stupid, and naïve and selfish. She could not bear to see the evidence of what wrath she had brought upon him. It was down to her.

WHEN WAR CAME TO LAUNDRY COTTAGE by Sarah Colliver

"I'm Aunty Vi, Jeremiah. And I'm going to visit you until you're all better. Don't worry about Sybil, she's in shock that's all, can't bear to think of you in pain. But she will find her feet in a minute, then she can sit here and hold your hand too."

Sybil pressed her back against the cold, white-washed wall, but slowly scanned his lifeless body, and her eyes settled on his crushed right arm hidden beneath a cage. His tall stature filled the bed, and tears swamped her eyes as she recalled him lifting her up to kiss his lips. She threw herself onto her knees beside the bed and buried her face in his blanket. Her heart shattered into pieces as she contemplated never being kissed by him again.

"I reckon he knows we are here, and if you love him the way you say, you'll stop all this nonsense now, and start thinking about someone other than yourself missy. He needs you, speak to him. Tell him he is going to be fine. I reckon it's your voice he'll want to hear, need. Not my croaky old words."

Sybil wiped her nose on her sleeve and took a deep breath. She forced open her eyes and stared at his mashed face, catching further sobs in her throat under the stern gaze of Aunty Vi. She leaned in, gently kissed his face, and whispered, "I'm here, right here, by your side. I'm so sorry I didn't listen to you."

Aunty Vi nodded reassuringly. "That's right my love. I told you Jeremiah, she would find her feet. It's a shock, because you're in a bad way, I'm not gonna lie, son. But if you can hear us, squeeze my hand, and if you can't manage that-wiggle your finger a little."

Sybil ran around the bed, and Aunty Vi ushered her into the chair, giving her his hand. "My love, can you hear me? Do you know we are here? It's me, Sybil." She leaned down and kissed his hand, over and over. "I'm here, we're here. This is my Aunty Vi. I hoped to introduce you in a more orthodox way, but then again, perhaps that was never going to be. We aren't exactly the 'norm' are we?"

Sybil froze, unsure if she imagined the slight movement, because it was what she so desperately wanted or if he really had managed it.

"Speak some more Sybil..." Aunty Vi whispered.

"My love, I need you to come back to me. You must recover, get better, our lives together have only just begun…"

His index finger pointed and retracted, prompting fresh tears from both bedside women. "Well, that's settled, he can hear us, so from now we are careful what we say. Positivity, and love is what he shall hear from our lips. Now, remember what the Sister said? He needs water, so come on, let's do our bit while we're here."

TWELVE

Sybil dialled the number for Deanwood House, "Hello, It's Sybil for Harriet please." Sybil hoped Harriet would get to the telephone before her money ran out, but she need not have worried as within a flash her voice was questioning her, as she answered.

"Where have you been? I feel utterly neglected Sybbie. Now I insist you come to dinner tonight. I have been waiting for you to call for days, since I sent my letter. Eight o'clock, and no excuses."

The line went dead, and she hadn't even managed to utter a single word, or even answer the invitation. To be fair it was more of an order, and clearly Harriet was not expecting rejection. It could be worse, if it were a hospital visiting night, she would have totally begrudged her dinner plans, but it was not Sister McMahon's shift, and they were only permitted on the nights when she was on duty. It was still very much a clandestine affair, to protect Jeremiah. Sybil would be compliant and attend the dinner, she still needed to pretend nothing was going on, and keep Harriet from suspecting anything.

She wandered home, reflecting on Jeremiah's slow recovery and what this meant. He could be shipped back to America if he recovered enough to be moved. Her heart sank at the thought, and the implications. Discharge from Army due to injury, unable to be a carpenter and earn a living, segregation? She shook her head and broke into a run, her anger surfacing and bubbling. She wanted to find those men, no not men, animals, who attacked him, and rip them apart.

WHEN WAR CAME TO LAUNDRY COTTAGE by Sarah Colliver

When her legs finally slowed and halted, she had run a mile past her house, and stood catching her breath by the neighbouring farm gate. A sleek black car stood behind the barn, only seen if you craned your neck and knew where to look. Voices and laughter echoed, and her instinct warned her to stay hidden, and so she cowered behind an old hay cart. Bobby Bradbury climbed into his car and drove away. He was the local black marketeer, and could lay his hands on most things, but nobody wanted to be seen associating with him.

Once the car had safely disappeared, Sybil sauntered along the lane to home, weary from her exertion. "Aunty Vi? Is the kettle on?"

Her familiar whistle danced on the air, as she scurried around with her newly made feather duster, "Well this works a treat! It's a new idea from a book Sheila has, using the wing feathers from the chickens to make feather dusters. I made five today! Testing them out, I am. Get in all the nooks and crannies lovely they do!"

WHEN WAR CAME TO LAUNDRY COTTAGE by Sarah Colliver

Sybil smiled at the enthusiasm radiating from her aunt. "They're wonderful, is there anything you can't do?" She planted a kiss on her forehead.

"I have decided, Ayda the chicken, is going to be our celebratory dinner, when we can get Jeremiah home. She's old now. Passed her laying days. Plus, I can make another duster out of her feathers!"

Sybil smiled. "What a lovely thought, him here with us." She could picture Jeremiah sat in the window seat, and her perched on his knee, peppering kisses over his face and neck. She wanted to believe this could happen, and the sentiment was beautiful, but it was a mess really, and she could not see any way forwards now. The only positive thing in the whole horrific situation, was that Jeremiah was left-handed, and the animals who attacked him, set about damaging his right. He may still be able to forge some kind of living, once he recovered fully. But that was a small mercy. "I have to go to dinner at the house tonight."

"Oh? Is that why you were summonsed to make that telephone call?"

Sybil nodded. "Not really in the mood, but I think she will start to ask too many questions if I don't keep up appearances, and I cannot risk anything else happening to him."

"Well, get yourself washed up, and dressed. You are a sight my girl, like you have been running for your life! Put your green dress on, get dolled up. Might perk you up a bit."

Sybil took a jug up to her room for a strip-wash. The cool water revived her a little, and as she pulled her hair up into pins, and swiped lipstick across her lips, she surveyed her reflection. Her sad eyes betrayed her otherwise glamourous appearance, but she was reassured that Harriet was far too wrapped up in herself, to see beyond the makeup and hair do. The last time she wore the green dress, Jeremiah called her the belle of the ball. She smoothed the fabric with her fingertips and longed for his kiss, his touch, his body on top of hers. She ached with every part of her being for him. Despite the impending doom which lingered, she also believed as strong as ever, that they were inevitable. They were meant to be together. He had come to England, to be with her, for their paths to cross, it was an entwined destiny. She hoped he was comfortable and safe in his hospital room, and that the contagion sign would keep his enemies at bay, for as long as it took her to figure out a way forward.

"You scrub up shinier than a shiny penny! A picture you are...now keep that smile painted on like your lipstick, and remember to, 'Be like Dad and keep Mum!' only, we aren't talking about Nazis sadly, but the enemy within, closer to home, eh?"

Sybil nodded and hugged her aunt, "Don't worry if I'm not home, it just means I've been pushed to stay at the house with Harriet. I know! I know! What *would* Dad say?"

Aunty Vi smiled, following along to the gate, to watch her disappear up the lane, with a wave. Sybil, worked to untangle her messy mind, and become Harriet's puppet once more, as her footsteps took her ever closer to the house.

On arrival she banged the heavy knocker, and waited, but there was no answer and so she pushed open the door. "Hello?" Her voice echoed.

WHEN WAR CAME TO LAUNDRY COTTAGE by Sarah Colliver

"Sybbie darling, in here, we're in the library!"

"Where's Ward?"

Harriet appeared in the gloomy panelled passage, "I've given her the week off, her sister is dreadfully ill in Cirencester. It was the right thing to do, but a bit bloody inconvenient really. Although she did leave enough food to feed a village. Cold meats and fresh bread tonight, I'm afraid." She led Sybil into the cosy library, where a group of high-ranking soldiers stood chatting with brandy. A familiar figure stood pulling out dusty books from the shelves, only to replace them and repeat it. She stared at the faces of the men and wondered if they had Jeremiah's blood on their hands. Her face flushed.

"Sybil!" Walt turned and pulled her into an embrace. "Harriet said you would be coming. It's so long since we caught up. How are you?"

Sybil understood his widened eyes but knew not to say anything about Jeremiah. She initially felt insulted by him thinking she could be that stupid, and then remembered her stupidity got the man she loved beaten to within an inch of his life. "Walt! Been dancing lately?"

"Nope! No-one can move like you!" He twirled her around and clasped her hand firmly.

"Right, everyone, let's have a drink! The girls aren't getting here until after nine, so no point waiting on them. Takes those land girls longer to get ready than the rest of us – on account of scrubbing the horse and cow muck away." Harriet threw back her head and laughed. Sybil shivered. She didn't even recognise her as the girl she met on the bus.

"Here Sybbie, Walter. Come on everyone, take a glass. To us. All of us. Bottoms up."

Sybil sipped the champagne and smiled at Walt, who seemed as uncomfortable as she felt. Perhaps a few glasses of bubbly would loosen her up a little, she felt wound up tight. She surveyed the company, none of whom were your average GI. They all had rank. Of course they did, Harriet wouldn't waste champagne on just anyone.

WHEN WAR CAME TO LAUNDRY COTTAGE by Sarah Colliver

"Sybbie's been so neglectful of late. Haven't you darling? Not spared me a minute. I've been here, lonesome." Harriet licked her lips and glanced at Walt, it was such a quick gesture and could have been easily missed. It was still a 'thing,' and this disappointed her. She thought more of him than that, but perhaps Harriet was right when she said that men have needs and cannot help themselves? That they are only after one thing. But not her Jeremiah, he refused when she offered herself to him. He could have taken her, and he didn't.

"Well, I do have to help my aunt, that's the whole purpose for me being here! There's always so much to do. I can't always be having fun with you, no matter how much I would like to."

Harriet beamed and kissed her on the cheek, "You do still love me, after all. I was beginning to wonder! Cheers everyone, to my Sybbie."

Sybil blushed with the attention of the room raising their glasses to her, but smiled and pretended to enjoy it. "Thanks so much everyone, really though!"

WHEN WAR CAME TO LAUNDRY COTTAGE by Sarah Colliver

"Now you handsome things, who wants to sit next to me and Sybbie at the table? We can't please everyone now, can we darling?" Harriet dramatically shrugged, and wiped her brow,

Slight panic crept in, what was she planning? No more pushing men towards her, she wasn't the same as Harriet, she didn't want that kind of attention. The veneer of her smile must have disappeared, because before she could react, or any of the ranked soldiers could respond to the open invitation to her, Walt was by her side. "Well, I must not let my dance partner slip away from me. Can I offer you my arm darling?"

Despite her recent disappointment in Walt, he became her rescuer, and she leant on him, preventing her weakened legs from buckling under her. "Perhaps you could grab some fresh air with me pre-dinner? A friendly smoke?" He winked.

Harriet beamed at his offer to Sybil, "Yes Sybbie, oh he really is such fabulous company, and knows how to put a woman at her ease. Do pop outside with him."

WHEN WAR CAME TO LAUNDRY COTTAGE by Sarah Colliver

Sybil's head reeled. Didn't she care that he was propositioning her? Was he even propositioning her or using it as an opportunity to be alone to talk? Before she could make sense of the situation, Walt and she were out on the back lawn, away from prying eyes. He lit them both a cigarette and passed one to her. "Go along with what I do or say. If I imply something is going on between us, laugh and nod. If it means we can have time to talk, it's worth it."

"But I will end up the talk of the village, people will think I am fooling around with a married man," She gasped.

"Better than the wrong people finding out the truth. I don't think you understand, Jeremiah is not safe here. There are people who want him dead." Walt's serious face gave her the chills.

"I didn't understand, until I saw the mess they made of him. Now I do. Animals."

Walt drew on his cigarette and stared upwards. "My wife died. Knocked over. Can you imagine? The world is on fire, Europe is amidst a massacre on a scale which the world has never seen, with bombs, guns, and mines. And my wife, safely tucked away- far from the war, is knocked over by some idiot who doesn't know when to stop drinking."

Sybil now understood why he was sleeping with Harriet. It was only sex. "I'm so sorry. I, I don't know what to say."

"Watch yourself with Harriet. She isn't all she makes out. You mustn't give her any inkling about Jeremiah, I don't know what she would do with that information."

"I haven't, I wouldn't. I know you cannot talk about what you have been through, seen, but..." Sybil gently clasped his hand.

"Don't ask me. You already surmise more than I want you to, you need to be careful, you don't know what you are mixing yourself up in. Now I need you to kiss me, let's make them think we have been a little friendly out here."

Sybil pulled him close, and kissed his lips, loosened his tie a little. He reached out and pulled a pin from her hair, "Fasten this as you go back in, and act giddy." Sybil was confused by this new turn of events, and wanted beyond anything else to protect Jeremiah, so decided to trust him.

"Before we go back, I want you to know that I am genuinely sorry about your wife. What was her name?"

"Louise."

"I'm so sorry about Louise. I cannot imagine how you must feel."

"Well, thanks honey. But, for now, let's put on a show, like when we danced, huh? I'm going to touch you throughout the meal and show you a hell of a lot of attention. So, respond naturally, you know you're safe with me, it's all an act."

Sybil allowed Walt to lead her back inside, where the full table erupted into cheers and whoops. Sybil fought to re-pin her hair, and Walt used a napkin to wipe away her lipstick from his mouth, as he pulled out her chair and gently tucked her under the table. He strategically placed her close to the end, away from the leering soldiers, eager for the arrival of the land girls. True to his word, he flirted and devoted his attention to her all evening. Sybil watched as Harriet lured in a new officer, possibly even a Major. He was much older, and plump with a ruddy face, and she couldn't imagine what she saw in him. Sybil still found decoding the uniforms and badges tricky, but by the end of the evening Harriet draped herself across his lap, and whatever his rank, he appeared to hang on her every word.

The arrival of the girls cranked up the dinner party, and as the champagne flowed, the gramophone threw out tunes, the white linen tablecloths became stages and dancefloors. Sybil stuck to Walt's side, and they danced until the room spun, their chemistry reignited by the hedonistic atmosphere. Sybil squealed as he flung her in the air and a light switched on in his eyes. Harriet sidled up to them, and whispered, "You can have your usual room Sybbie, have fun, let loose a little. You two are great together." Sybil smiled and nodded as Walt pulled her away in a spin and through the door.

WHEN WAR CAME TO LAUNDRY COTTAGE by Sarah Colliver

"Where are we going? Walt?" But she remembered his voice in her head, 'trust me, it's all an act, you want to protect Jeremiah at all costs?' and allowed him to lead her up to her room. They would probably just sleep it off, and pretend things had 'gone on.'

He thrust open the door, and pulled her in, slamming it shut behind them. Sybil caught her breath, and kicked off her shoes, which were pinching her toes, relieved that the pretence could be shelved for a while. She yawned and peeked out of the curtain. It was a full moon. The warmth of Walt's breath on her neck startled her, and he began to playfully nibble her ear. "Dance with me."

"What are you doing?" Sybil pushed him back. "We don't need to pretend in here. No one can see us silly."

"Dance with me. You know how good we are together, it's only a dance."

"But there's no music."

"Who needs music?" He pulled her close and held her tightly, moving his feet to imaginary music. She could feel him instantly aroused as he pushed closer to her.

"Walt?"

"Louise, I've missed you so much."

"WALT! IT'S ME SYBIL!" Panic rose, and he had the faraway look in his eyes, as though he were lost. She knew she must bring him back and fought to free herself from his firm grip. "STOP IT! PLEASE WALT!" She slapped him hard across the face, and he pulled away. For a moment she thought he may hit her back, but instead his eyes flickered.

"Oh fuck! I'm sorry! What the fuck just happened?"

Sybil was unsure whether to flee or stay put. She gingerly moved to where her shoes lay and slipped them on. "You scared me."

"I would never want to hurt you. I don't know what happened. The drink, the dancing, Louise..."

"I want to go home now."

WHEN WAR CAME TO LAUNDRY COTTAGE by Sarah Colliver

"How can I make this okay? Sybil? I promise you- this will never happen again. I am so ashamed."

Sybil was at a loss to know what to believe, she had trusted him, had reason to, after all he had done for them. And from their first encounter, she had known he carried a darkness, heavy secrets which stole his peace. Six months ago, the Sybil she was then, would have run as fast as she could. But something in the pit of her stomach, encouraged her to stay.

"Come and lay down. You're done in." She pulled the covers back, and pushed him onto the bed, removing his shoes and dropping them to the floor. She tucked him in, and then lay on top of the covers next to him, pulling a blanket from the chair over her legs. It occurred to her, that in the way Jeremiah was scarred from his beating, Walt's damage was not visible, but they were deep wounds non the less. Sybil rhythmically stroked his hair until he fell asleep. Sleep however did not come to Sybil. Her mind raced, unable to make sense of everything which had gone on in the evening. And as she attempted to untangle her thoughts, she witnessed the unease which attacked Walt even as he slept, as his body flinched, and his arms flayed. They say sleep is escape, but what happens to you when sleep only brings your enemy closer?

THIRTEEN

Aunty Vi bustled around the compact kitchen, sweeping and dusting with gusto. Their chatter seemed to power her, like a wind-up toy. "It's a web of intrigue for sure, no wonder you are all a tizz! I had an idea she was up to no good…"

"Yes, but it doesn't make sense, none of it. I get it, she has a big mouth and a lot of contact with many GIs, so it wouldn't be ideal for her to be shouting about Jeremiah. But the more I think about it, the more there seems to be to it…and what are Walt's secrets? What is haunting him?"

"We're all haunted by something," Aunty Vi pondered leaning on the wispy old broom.

"I know. I need to be on guard with Harriet, I no longer feel safe with her intentions. I wasn't sure what she had in mind for me at that dinner party, and was so relieved Walt was there, I think he saved me from a delicate situation." She decided against revealing her 'close call' with him. Aunty wouldn't understand.

"Hmm. Well, we have a lot to try and do before our visit tonight. So, you get on with outside, those chickens need a feed and the veggie beds weeding, I'll start in here. Will you look at the dust, and that floor needs a proper scrub. At six we will have supper. I want to take Jeremiah a little cake tonight, I managed to acquire a little sugar, by swapping a few eggs, and have enough to make a small one for him. We can take a bottle of my ginger ale too. Home comforts can lift the spirits. If we can sneak them past Sister."

Since hospital volunteers do not carry bags, they had to be a little inventive when sneaking contraband into Jeremiah. Aunty Vi suggested the idea of strapping the bottle of ale between two garters on Sybil's thigh, whilst she smuggled the cake in grease-proof parchment in her outer pocket. It was exciting to slip it past the eager eyes of Sister McMahon, who noticed everything on her ward.

On arrival Jeremiah sat upright. "Good evening, ladies," he laughed as they removed his treats from their bodies. "What's going on here?"

Sybil lifted the bottle to his lips, and he sipped the liquid gratefully. "It tastes like a little piece of heaven, after having water and tea for all these weeks. Thank you."

"It's Aunty Vi's recipe, you approve?"

"You are an angel Aunty Vi."

She swiftly but gently delivered a kiss to his forehead. "You charmer, Mr Thomas! Lovely to hear your voice returning, especially when you have such lovely things to say. Now I am going to nip out of here for a moment, I will be back in a jiffy." Aunty Vi crept out of the door, past the Sister.

"You brought me back. My love, come here, let me hold you."

WHEN WAR CAME TO LAUNDRY COTTAGE by Sarah Colliver

Sybil perched on the side of the bed and kissed him tenderly on the lips. Her body tingled at his touch. "I know I couldn't bear to live without you, but I must say something, I'm so, so sorry my love. I should've listened to you, and I refused, I pushed you to come to the party and it's my fault..."

Jeremiah pressed his finger to her lips and silenced her words. He pulled her in close and kissed her again, deeper, his mouth hungry for hers. Their hearts raced, a delicious stolen moment confirmed that they were so right together, meant to be, and nothing and no one was going to prevent it, whatever it took.

"Now I must speak. Remember when we first met, when you dropped the log on your toe, and hopped around the garden? Before that moment, I existed, but I wasn't alive. You brought me to life. You gave me life. Hope. I know you are meant for me. I don't know how this can happen, but it must. I love you, Sybil."

Sybil's sobs mingled with his fresh tears, as they declared their love for each other.

WHEN WAR CAME TO LAUNDRY COTTAGE by Sarah Colliver

The door swung open, "This is improper, and I shall remain in here until your Aunt returns to the room. I shall have no shenanigans on my ward."

They both giggled, but Sybil clung to Jeremiah's hand.

"Thank you, Sister. For everything you have done and continue to do for us. We cannot thank you enough."

"I'm simply doing my job. Right, I can hear your aunt returning now. Oh, and I hope the cake and ale went down well. But please keep it quiet, or chaos will ensue around here." She winked and straightened her dress before sweeping out onto the ward.

"Well, I don't know If you two are laughing or crying?"

"Both!"

"So have they said anything about your recovery love?" Aunty Vi moved up to his damaged hand, still hidden beneath the cage.

"Well, they have said they want to try a new operation on it, which could improve it a little, but it will never fully function. It is more of a practice for them I think, and they'll need to monitor me for six weeks afterwards. I don't hold out much hope, but my thoughts are if they operate, I stay longer."

"Yes! You must let them operate. It could buy us time." Sybil kissed his cheek.

"So, I don't think I'm jumping the gun, I can see the devotion from you both, never seen the like before. So, I assume marriage is on your mind? We must figure out how to make that happen? Not sure it can, not right now, anyway. But we should try and find the way to keep you here at least."

"It's impossible I'm afraid, you must have the permission of a senior rank, and they have been instructed not to give it. I really don't know any way around it."

"I could come back with you?"

"Home? Are you crazy my love? You don't understand."

"No, I don't. None of it. Why two people can't be together?"

WHEN WAR CAME TO LAUNDRY COTTAGE by Sarah Colliver

"Where I come from, you couldn't even share the sidewalk with me. And marry me? Jeez, it's no good, it just can't happen, I reckon hell would freeze over before it did. I don't know. Only way I can think of to stay, is if I get offered a job and lodging here, and someone takes me on. Fights to keep me. But who's going to do that now? I'm useless."

"One step at a time. First you need to get this operation done. That gives us at least six weeks to sort something out."

"Aunty Vi is right, we can't give up, we must find a way. We already have a gift of six weeks, can we tell Sister now, that you want to go ahead with it? What if they come for you, ship you home before it's arranged? We must secure it now. I can't lose you I can't!"

"Hey, Sybil, my love, hush now." He lifted her hand to his mouth and rubbed it across his lips. "My guess is that she suggested me as a candidate in the first place. She has a soft spot for me you know. Better watch out…"

"If you weren't already laid up in bed, I would be giving you a piece of my mind Mr. But since you are, I'm going to kiss you instead." Sybil kissed him and then kissed him again before offering him the ginger ale, which he gratefully swallowed.

"Now, let's call her in and agree to this operation. Then you can both go home and get some sleep, you look exhausted."

FOURTEEN

Neither Sybil, nor Aunty Violet could settle to anything on the day of the operation. It would hopefully improve Jeremiah's hand, but also ensure he remained for another six weeks so he could be monitored, and the results studied. Sister McMahon was proving to be his guardian angel. So far Sybil had ignored two dinner invites, from Harriet, claiming to be poorly, but now she was playing her birthday promise letter, and demanding they get together.

WHEN WAR CAME TO LAUNDRY COTTAGE by Sarah Colliver

"You must go, remember that you are doing it for him. It's pretend, that's all. Theres nothing can be done for him right now anyway." Aunty Vi's words of encouragement stung a bit, she did not understand how difficult Harriet had become.

"I know. I will telephone her, get it all sorted." Sybil pulled on her jacket and shivered a little as she left, it was chillier now, and soon there would be frost on the ground. They had been busy picking windfall apples locally and collecting the blackberries for preserving. A group of them pooled forces, like with the pig they all fed and would share at slaughter. More hands make light work, and many more preservatives to go around. It was quite an enjoyable experience, as they would gather at one of the larger kitchens, and chatter away as they chopped and stirred. There were amazing old tales told, of the countryside and beliefs held. Mrs Duberly would insist on reading their tea leaves, turning their cup three times before decrypting the soggy, overused leaves. They would all silence to hear each reading in turn, and Sybil was fascinated by the age-old tradition.

WHEN WAR CAME TO LAUNDRY COTTAGE by Sarah Colliver

If the war ended tomorrow, Sybil would stay with Aunty Vi. She felt increasingly like a country girl at heart and missed little of the old city life. Chaotic, dirty, and noisy.

She dialled the house, and Harriet answered, "Yes?"

"Still no Ward?"

"Well, that's a nice greeting! I take it you are all better from your frightful cold?"

"Yes, thank you. Sorry I haven't seen you, but I really didn't want to spread the lurgy, it was a horrible one."

"I appreciate that, no one wants lurgy's. Now, how about you and I go out tomorrow? I have an invite to a party and need a female companion."

"Where is it?"

"Don't worry about that, make sure you come glammed up. Grant and I will collect you at seven, and do wear stockings this time darling, if you don't have any please call in and I can sort some out for you, I only ever wear mine once. Seven tomorrow evening, bye darling."

It was akin to having an officer in charge, giving the orders and rendezvous times. Once again, she was to be Harriet's sidekick, but on reflection it may seem odd, her arriving alone, and it is always easier with a friend. It wouldn't be for much longer either. Once Jeremiah was safe, all of this could stop. The pretence could end, and she would once again be in control of her own destiny.

Sybil leant against the wall of the garden and checked her watch, it was gone seven, and she really was not in the mood for Harriet. Sister McMahon had sent news via her son, who rode to the house with a letter:

Patient is doing well, in recovery and on special ward for monitoring progress. New arrangements to be made for visiting. Await my contact before coming in.

Sister M

So that was that and the waiting game commenced. She must remember to be grateful for those helping to keep him safe, and not mope about the no visiting rule for now. The roar of an engine jolted her from deep thought, and she automatically stood tall and smiled. Grant stopped the car and ran to open the door, nodding his head, "Miss."

"Thank you, Grant," she answered, and climbed in beside Harriet who was smoking a cigarette in a sleek black holder. "New look?"

"This? Oh, a little, gift from an admirer. You wearing that bloody green dress again? Really."

"It's the only one I have! Anyway, I love it."

"At least you have stockings on this time, and they aren't too shabby. Now, we are off to a base, and I need support, darling. And you, are it."

Sybil stifled a sigh. She knew exactly what she meant. "Who are you after this time? I have lost count."

"Well, really. Fine one to talk, I mean how's Walter these days?"

Sybil blushed. She forgot that Harriet would assume they were lovers. "I haven't seen him since your dinner party."

WHEN WAR CAME TO LAUNDRY COTTAGE by Sarah Colliver

Harriet raised her eyebrows and flicked ash onto the floor. It landed on Sybil's shoe and marked it. She licked her finger to try and rub it away.

"Well, it may well be your lucky night, because he might, I stress might, be there. So here, have a little something to loosen yourself up, you seem so very uptight these days." Harriet took a hip flask from her clasp bag and offered it to Sybil.

Sybil thought about declining, but decided perhaps she was right; she should loosen up a little if she wanted to get through the evening and swiped it from her hand. She swallowed the burning liquid and drained it dry.

"There's none left for me, Sybbie, really!"

"Can I have a smoke please, too?"

"Of course, here."

Sybil wanted the evening over and done with, as painlessly as possible. "You know that you can only use my birthday promise once, and that this is that one time?"

WHEN WAR CAME TO LAUNDRY COTTAGE by Sarah Colliver

"Yes, I know that. But I would have liked to think you came along to be with me because we are friends? What has happened, that I must emotionally blackmail you these days in to spending time with me?"

Sybil drew on her cigarette and realised her pretence was slipping and she needed to take back control. "Sorry Harri, I haven't been myself lately, that damn lurgy knocked the stuffing out of me, that's all."

"Right then, pep up lovely, and let's have a jolly old time, but darling, please don't call me Harri, it's a man's name and I don't care for it."

Sybil nodded, smiled with gritted teeth, and dropped her cigarette to the floor, crushing it beneath her heel. The countryside sped past them, as they raced through the lanes, to God knows where.

Sybil smiled until her face hurt and wished she were laying in the arms of Jeremiah.

Grant slowed the car on arrival and Harriet instructed him, "Thank you. Now, you park up around the corner there, and wait."

"Thanks Grant." Sybil smiled.

"You really are too familiar with the hired help darling. Come on, this way I believe." Harriet's momentary scowl turned into a sarcastic smile.

A large Georgian mansion house, four times the size of Deanwood, loomed above them, and a uniformed soldier stood in front of the door. "This way please ladies," he spoke in a cockney accent and opened the grand door wide enough for them to gain access but quick enough not to break the black out. They stepped into a cavernous entrance hall, which echoed with every sound. It was imposing and clinical and Sybil shivered. Another soldier was on hand to direct guests and ushered them to the left where the buzz of a large function sounded. Loud music played, but it was not live, just a gramophone.

The bar was jam-packed with people, dimly lit and the entire room panelled, with shutters tight to the windows. Sybil imagined it as a giant coffin, hemmed in by all that wood. She did not like it. It was a mix of American and British military, and it seemed anyone who was of importance. Harriet grabbed hold of Sybil and began to weave her way through the throng of people, who all sounded frightfully posh. Sybil fought the urge to escape and sit in the car with Grant, where she would be more comfortable.

"Major! So wonderful to see you." Harriet kissed a moustached man on both cheeks, and Sybil immediately recognised him as the man she had been draped across at her dinner party.

"Harriet, Sybil, lovely to see you both again, please allow me to introduce you to my wife…"

Harriet's mask slipped as she took in his words, clearly not expecting his wife to attend, but only for a moment, before she took Lady Barton's hand, "Absolutely delightful to meet with you, the Major has told us all about you, hasn't he Sybbie darling?"

WHEN WAR CAME TO LAUNDRY COTTAGE by Sarah Colliver

Sybil smiled, nodded in agreement, and suppressed the urge to laugh at the Majors newly scarlet face. "Oh yes, we've heard so much about you!"

"Come on Sybbie, let's get a drink, oh there are some canapes over there too. It's like a giant game of sardines!" Harriet yanked Sybil away from the Major and his wife and snatched two glasses of bubbles for them on the way. "Well, that was awkward! I do wish people would give me some kind of warning concerning wives appearing unexpectedly."

Sybil sipped her champagne and fought to keep the crowd from knocking her drink over them. "What is this party for? Why so many people?"

"Absolutely no idea darling, I abide by one important rule: never pass on an invitation. Can you stay here for a moment, I must find the powder room."

"I can come too?"

"Darling Sybbie, stay here for a moment, let anyone who asks know I am powdering my nose."

WHEN WAR CAME TO LAUNDRY COTTAGE by Sarah Colliver

Sybil swapped her empty glass for a new one, and attempted to blend into the shadows, keen not to draw attention to herself. Why were they even there? The rowdy crowd became more unruly with every drink, and all Sybil wanted to do was leave. What was taking Harriet so long? She checked her watch; she had been gone for fifteen minutes. Enough was enough, what if she left her there? How would she get home, she did not even know where she was or anyone who was there except for the Major.

She drained her glass, took another and headed through the door nearest to her, which Harriet had used. It was an anteroom with a quieter group discussing the war, and so she continued through one room after another until she reached a closed door. With no sign of the powder room or Harriet, she pushed on through, closing each door behind her. Finally, a room without lights, and she realised that she must have come too far. She was about to turn and leave when voices raised in the room ahead, so she crept up to the door and pressed her ear against it. A man and a woman, and a heated discussion. Or a stolen moment of passion. The memory flashed into her mind of the last time she witnessed a stolen moment, near the little log cabin, where Harriet was pleasured by a British officer. She blushed at the recollection. She should not be listening and pulled away from the door, suddenly fearing she may be caught snooping.

"You can't get away with this now Harriet." The voice shouted and Sybil gasped. "I've known for some time, I just needed proof. So, I sat and I waited."

"Darling, I think you've had too much to drink. You're having one of your funny turns."

"Don't try that one on me." Walt seethed.

"Get your hands off me, or I'll scream!"

Sybil pushed open the door and screamed, "Get off her!"

Walt had Harriet pinned in the corner. Her hands behind her back with his one hand, his other around her neck and his knee in her abdomen. He turned, "You don't know what you're doing, you know nothing about this Sybil. Leave, no even better, get the Major!"

Harriet wriggled a hand free and pushed Walt hard, he stumbled backwards, and Harriet threw herself at the door, slamming it shut.

"Harriet, what's happening, are you ok?" Her mind flashed to Walt's last 'turn' when he thought she was his wife. Who knows what he would have done if she hadn't slapped him.

"Fucks sake Sybil, you don't know what you've done." Walt shouted.

"Don't listen to him Sybbie, he isn't in his right mind. He's been trying it on with me, pestering me, won't leave me alone and because I refuse him, he's become delusional. Accusing me of all sorts." Harriet stepped backwards until she reached the closed door and locked it, placing the key in her pocket.

"Don't believe a word that bitch utters Sybil, I told you before, she isn't who she makes out to be."

"Oh, do shut up. Says he. And who are you, Walt? Poor, poor Walt. Little wifey died, so let's all cry together, eh?"

"Don't you speak about my wife. Fuck you!"

"What the hell is going on? What are you both doing?" Sybil thought her head would explode, and suddenly the alcohol consumed began to take effect. "Is this some lovers tiff?"

"Grow up Sybbie. Life isn't all about love and being a good girl for Aunty. It's about war, death, glory, and picking the winning side."

Sybil grew more frustrated by the moment, at the stalemate situation they found themselves in. "Well, what next then? Why are we locked in here now? Tell me what is going on?"

"He is a spy."

Sybil laughed. And then she stopped and stared at Harriet's serious face. Suddenly the darkness Walt carried, disturbed sleep and secrets made sense. She believed her. "Oh my God."

WHEN WAR CAME TO LAUNDRY COTTAGE by Sarah Colliver

"She's a spy." Walt uttered the words as though it were an everyday phrase.

"Really need to work on your technique." Harriet moved towards Walt and removed a small revolver from her belt.

Sybil did not know who to believe, what was real or if she was victim to a vivid dream enhanced by alcohol, but she knew she couldn't watch Walt be murdered. She flung herself at Harriet, grabbing a cane from the stand beside her and with the greatest force she could muster slammed it across her hand. The gun fell to the floor. Sybil sighed with relief amidst Harriet's screams.

"You fucking little bitch!"

Suddenly, Walt loomed above with her gun, pointing it at her head.

"Oh, for the love of God." Sybil edged away from her position next to Harriet, unsure of his state of mind.

"She is the spy. She is feeding back information from all the men she beds. She sends coded messages to the enemy from somewhere in Deanwood House, which I haven't managed to find yet. She isn't 21 either, try 30."

"Ouch darling, now that hurts, I'm 25."

Sybil could not speak. What could she say?

"You were part of her lovely little cover story I'm afraid. Got caught in the crossfire. You, Harriet, are very much sought after by important people I know, but how tempting it is, to shoot you here, right now."

"Please don't. Surely, she must have loads of useful information?" Sybil felt panicked, still unsure of the unfolding situation. "Did you check the middle of the maze, there's a locked shed there."

"Sounds like a perfect hiding place to me. And you, lady, better thank your lucky stars Sybil's here, because if it was only us, I don't fancy your chances much."

Sybil wandered to the window and peeped around the blackout. As suspected Grant was waiting nearby. A perfectly planned escape route. "Why don't we tie her up, and bundle her out of the window, and take her to, well I don't know where? Where do you take Nazi spies?" Sybil was already removing her stockings when a shot echoed, and Harriet screamed.

"Why did you do that?" Sybil yelled at Walt, afraid.

"It's only her leg. To stop her escaping, easier to transport."

"Sybbie darling, help me. Please, he's a lunatic," Harriet sobbed. Sybil pondered for a moment, was that sympathy she felt for her? She pushed it aside whilst tying one stocking around Harriet's mouth at the back of her head and bound her hands with the other.

Walt picked up the tiny camera, built within her make up compact, which had been dropped in their scuffle onto the grand oak desk, and put the classified documents back into the hidden drawer. "Thank God these won't make it into enemy hands. If I hadn't caught her today, I dread to think what devastation this woman would have been responsible for."

Walt lifted Harriet onto his shoulder as she wriggled and writhed, and then threw her out of the window, where her fall was broken by a laurel bush. Then Sybil and he climbed out.

"Let's get out of here, quickly." He dragged her from the bushes and picked her back up, as they ran towards the car. Grant jumped out of his seat startled by the commotion.

"What the hell?"

"Get back in your seat and do your job, or I'll shoot you. I shot her and will do the same to you without hesitation. Both of us can drive so we don't need you in this equation. You are a luxury for now."

Grant started up the engine, and drove away from the mansion house, heading to the main road, his hands shaking. "Where do you want me to drive to?"

Walt, deep thought, was silent for a moment. "Left out of here and keep going for now." Harriet squealed. "Shut up bitch." He pointed the gun back at Harriet, and then re-aimed at Grant, who appeared shaken and his face ashen.

WHEN WAR CAME TO LAUNDRY COTTAGE by Sarah Colliver

"Where are we going?" Sybil asked, wondering if anyone would be allowed to know such top-secret information and fearing for her own safety.

He said nothing. Sybil watched Grant, hoping he would not pass out in shock or crash with fear, and something glistened and caught her eye. He was easing, ever so slowly, a revolver from his pocket. She needed to warn Walt. But how?

"Walter? You know Louise was killed by a drunk driver? What would you do to that driver now?"

A single shot through the back of Grant's head sent his brains splattering everywhere. Sybil wiped them from her face and grabbed hold of the steering wheel, she couldn't die now, Jeremiah needed her. As Walt fought to pull Grants body into the back, Sybil wriggled her way into the driving seat, and slowed the car down, bringing it to a stop.

"Why have you stopped? Keep going."

"I need to see where I'm going." She removed her petticoat and wiped the mess from the windscreen. "How do I know you aren't going to do that to me?

I've worked out that where you need to go must be so secret, I'm not authorised. I don't want to die."

"Listen, keep driving, and leave the rest to me. We'll swap when we get nearer. You are safe. I told you that you never ever need to fear me and meant it. Okay?"

Sybil re-started the car, and drove on, wondering how on earth she could be covered in Grant's blood and brains, with Harriet shot and tied up in the back of a car she was now driving.

"You know I haven't actually properly learned how to drive?"

"At this point Sybbie, I don't think that really matters."

"Please don't call me Sybbie, I hate it."

"Noted."

    Sybil was flagging and hoped she wouldn't need to drive much further.

"Okay, pull in here. We need to swap." Take this and point it at her. I'm sorry but you need to sit with them both. Don't make eye contact with her, she will try and convince you to untie her. Do not. And don't say anything because she can hear you."

Sybil nodded and climbed into the tiny space in the back, her mind whirling at the absurdity, of a dead body strewn across the lap, of the bound and wide-eyed Harriet. They were all covered in blood. She held the gun with both hands to steady her aim, as the car pulled away, and headed off into the dark night.

At the first barrier, Walt showed an ID card, which prompted the second guard to radio ahead for the remaining three barriers to be lifted, enabling them to speed through the extensive grounds, and pull into what appeared to be an aircraft hangar.

The car stopped, and Sybil swallowed the bile which crept into her throat. What was going to happen to her? Before she could come up with a single solution, Walt exited the car, which became immediately surrounded by pointed guns. Sybil swallowed her vomit and stifled her tears of panic, unsure whether to drop the gun aimed at Harriet and put her hands up or remain pointing it at her.

"Sybil, don't panic, drop the gun over on to the front seat, and climb out of the car with your hands up."

She wanted to question him, why did she need to put her hands in the air? She wasn't a criminal, this was insane. But fear stole her voice, and she followed his instructions. As she straightened up, her legs threatened to buckle, and Walt yanked her back away from the car. She was whisked through a door into a large echoing room.

Although she wasn't hand-cuffed, it felt as though she was under arrest and her heart leapt into her mouth. Panic swept across her in beads of sweat. No one knew where she was, anything could happen to her. What about Jeremiah? If she weren't around, he would be shipped back, and they would never be together. He needed her. That single thought stiffened her resolve, and she straightened herself up, and pushed away the fear which had threatened to disable her. She could handle this if it were over with swiftly and she could return home.

FIFTEEN

Sybil yawned and checked her wristwatch; it was gone eleven o'clock. Blood splatters clung to the watch face, and she wiped them away with her stained dress. The room was chilly, she was glad of her jacket which kept the shivers away. Walt told her to stay put, they would debrief her as soon as possible. At midnight, an immaculately dressed woman, in a pristine white satin blouse with glossy black hair, brought in a cup of sweet tea, with a reassuring nod and smile, but the waiting was agonising.

She reflected on the evenings revelations, and recalled her encounters with Harriet and what clues she may have missed. Their initial meeting on the bus, instigated by Harriet. The almost suffocating friendship she forged, with a plethora of gifting, food for Aunty and delicious meals. The many gatherings with a stream of uniforms, and her obsession with Walt and she getting together, had she known he was undercover? Lucky guess? An image of Harriet kneeling on the floor, naked, whilst Walt slept at Deanwood House, sprung into her mind. She must have been rooting through his possessions, so maybe she was suspicious? Or trying to see exactly who he was, and what info he may have. The fact that Harriet, a simple nanny, had so much power in the house without anyone batting an eye lid, and the flowers, who were they from? Perhaps she was in a sort of relationship with the owner of Deanwood House, Richard Bentley? She must have been using her sexual dalliances to extract information, blackmail?

The questions swam around her head until she felt dizzy and exhausted. There were so many clues now she thought about it all, she felt as though she had been bumbling around with her eyes closed. No, not closed, focussed on falling in love, and hiding the fact. She had her own secrets. And anyway, who in their right minds would ever, in a million years think that there would be spies, in sleepy Dewton? It would NEVER have occurred to her that Harriet was anything of such, a loose woman? Yes. Vain and bossy? Yes. But a spy? It was beyond anything her mind could comprehend. All of the Ministry of War posters weren't so far-fetched or scaremongering after all. In fact, they were spot on to suggest being careful who we talk to and what we say. The enemy really were embedded among us. She should know that better than anyone. Jeremiah was employed by his enemy, and had no choices, rights, or freedom. It made her blood boil. How dare they use them to fight oppression, and fascism when they promoted such dark ideology within their own camp?

"Sybil? You still holding up?" Walt's voice was familiar and comforting. "You seem to have had an unexpected turn of events." He squeezed her shoulder and slumped into the seat in front of her. He lit a cigarette and offered the packet, Sybil obliged, and inhaled deeply.

"I don't know what to say really." Sybil stared at Walt, he had a fire in his eyes, despite the heavy bags beneath them. "There's so many...I mean, I don't know what to think, or say...it's not something you expect to happen? I thought she was one of those self-obsessed rich girls, who had grown up with everything she ever wanted. You know, used to getting her own way. I would never have imagined this...but who would?" She scratched her head and drew on her cigarette.

WHEN WAR CAME TO LAUNDRY COTTAGE by Sarah Colliver

"You held up well, minimum disruption caused to the public. I have already had the room unlocked and cleaned, so everyone at the party is non-the-wiser. When it came down to it, you kept your head and you got on with it. You could have screamed, frozen or panicked, but you didn't. Let's not forget that you saved my life too."

"I did?" There was too much to process.

"Grant would have finished me off if you hadn't acted so quickly. And then who knows how this story would have ended. Well done!"

Sybil blushed. At least she felt redemption for all the missed clues and being taken in by Harriet's act.

"You know that there will be a sort of debrief with you in the next ten minutes, and you will be asked to sign the official secrets act. This isn't a choice, you understand? You can never discuss any of this with anyone, so we will need a story to cover Harriet and Grants disappearance. Deanwood House will be requisitioned for military use, a hospital of some kind for recuperation. I can't discuss what will happen to all those involved behind the scenes, a need-to-know basis you understand. But everything will be explained to you by my colleagues."

Sybil nodded. It felt like a final farewell, and she would be sad in a way. He was a good man, a friend, despite his demons. "Walt, if that is even your name, was any of it real? I mean, our friendship?"

He stood and gently lifted Sybil from her chair, pulling her in tight to his chest. Her tears flowed, and her body expelled the pent-up emotions as he held her.

"It's okay to let it out." He rubbed her back rhythmically, until her sobs subsided. "Come on honey, you felt that connection when we danced? You can't fake that kind of chemistry. In another world, you and I would be great friends Sybil." He passed her a handkerchief and she smiled through her tears. "But for now, it is goodbye." Walt kissed her on each cheek, and then her hands. "It's been an absolute pleasure, you are a beautiful soul, and much, much stronger than you realise. Now, please, sit back down, and they will be in shortly. So long Sybil."

WHEN WAR CAME TO LAUNDRY COTTAGE by Sarah Colliver

"Bye, Walt." Suddenly overwhelmed and too tired to think straight, all she wanted to do was sleep. To curl up in a tight ball, beneath the weight of the ancestral quilt at Laundry Cottage. Her exhausted brain seemed incapable of any clear thinking, like a steam engine which had been over-stoked.

She watched him disappear through the door from where he came and turned back to face the desk and window. It was still dark and afforded no view. Walt's cigarette packet caught her eye. She pulled it towards her, grateful for something to pass the time while she waited.

When she arrived home, it was mid-afternoon, and Aunty Vi's familiar whistle carried across the garden where she was busy feeding the chickens. Sybil paused at the gate for a moment, breathing in the crisp air, and soaking up the wonderful safety of home. She felt rooted to Laundry Cottage now, it was where she was meant to be, she knew it. And she was grateful for her new life, which ironically the war had brought to her.

WHEN WAR CAME TO LAUNDRY COTTAGE by Sarah Colliver

Her dress and jacket, cleaned but damp, no longer bore Grant's blood, and although pale and tired, she could easily pretend she was returning from a night of dancing. She kicked off her shoes and bent to pick them up, her feet really did ache, and her body longed for bed.

"Aunty Vi! Shall we put the kettle on?" She called as she rounded the corner to the back door.

"Morning love. Ooh, someone's done in." Aunt Vi followed her into the kitchen and washed her hands in the porcelain bowl. "You hungry? I expect that Miss Harriet has fed you up, as usual. Here give me those." She gently took her shoes and placed them by the door.

Sybil was beyond hunger, and could barely string a sentence together, but managed a weary smile. As if she was in on the secret, Aunty Vi guided her up the stairs to her bed, and hung up her coat. Not a word about 'out galivanting until all hours when there was work to do,' or 'what would her father think.' "No point in even making that tea just yet, as I think you are too far gone to enjoy it, and we mustn't be wasteful," she spoke softly as she tucked Sybil up beneath the heavy quilt, fully clothed. Sybil was too exhausted to thank her, but her last thought before drifting away was of gratitude and warmth.

Sybil awoke to darkness and her parched throat begged for relief, as did her bladder. As she found herself still fully clothed beneath the bedding, she decided to boil the kettle whilst she popped to the outhouse, and crept downstairs to avoid waking Aunty Vi. Her visit outside was as swift as she could manage, and after washing her hands, with the jug and bowl, she mashed the days old tealeaves, so that her tea could only loosely be described as such, more accurately boiled water with a hint of something. Her dry throat eased, and she settled into the chair by candlelight.

Warm embers glowed in the fire, and then her mind kicked in. The myriad of thoughts rushed to her all at once, and she had to remind herself that this all needed to be buried, because she could not talk to anyone about it. She decided to brush up on the

WHEN WAR CAME TO LAUNDRY COTTAGE by Sarah Colliver

recent version of events, so that she could act more casually when it inevitably cropped up. That the party was a last Hurrah for Harriet, who left afterwards to return to London, as Deanwood House was being requisitioned for the war effort. That ticked that box. If Aunty asked about Walt, then easy enough to vaguely mention that he may have been posted overseas. A rumour would be spread about Grant running off with stolen heirlooms, which the gossip mongers of the village would devour, and Ward would stay in Cirencester, once her debrief and involvement discovered. Perhaps Sybil would never know if she had been involved or not, but potentially, there was a big chance she was in on it all, considering the level of involvement from Grant. Surely, she had to be aware. The village would assume Ward was staying with her sister, and due to the requisition, there was no longer a role for her anyway.

Her mind flashed back to the bullet entering Grant's head and she winced, as she wiped imaginary blood from her face. It was all because of meeting Harriet, or whatever her name was, that she had become embroiled in the whole sorry affair.

WHEN WAR CAME TO LAUNDRY COTTAGE by Sarah Colliver

Footsteps grew louder and the door opened, "Aunty Vi?" The clock on the mantle chimed 3.

"So, you're awake? Left you to sleep, now, that teapot need topping up? And let's stoke that fire, eh?"

Sybil felt pangs of guilt at leaving the fire to almost die, and hopped out of her chair and began to rekindle it. "You sit, I'll sort the tea."

Aunty Vi seemed weary but had a sparkle in her eye. "You've been out cold since midday my girl! Must have been wiped out. I've been to the hospital, I have. Seen our Jeremiah. He's doing ever so well, but not well enough to be moved, if you get my drift. That Sister McMahon is a force to be reckoned with. Here."

Aunty Vi handed a note to Sybil with a smile. "Save it for when we go to bed, you can enjoy it on your own, every word. That boy is special you know, I can see why you feel the way you do. Reckon the Sister feels the same. At least we are all on the same page. Now, let's have a cuppa before we head up, eh? There's still a day's work ahead of us, and we need to get some sleep."

WHEN WAR CAME TO LAUNDRY COTTAGE by Sarah Colliver

Sybil pressed the letter to her lips, understanding that it was a note from Jeremiah, and smiled. The fact that Aunty Vi had visited him alone, not let him down, made her heart sing with joy, because this meant he had a place at Laundry Cottage, if they could ever find a way to make it happen. "Was he really alright? Didn't he wonder where I was?"

"Of course he missed you! Why do you think we had to ask Sister for paper, so he could write you that. He could only manage a few words, it's very early days. I explained it couldn't be helped; you going out. He understood, but missed seeing you, that's all."

"It's a long story, too long for tonight, but my partying days at Deanwood are over now, and I couldn't be more relieved to be honest."

Aunty Vi nodded and squeezed her hand. "Think I'll take my cup up to my bed. Night, night. Lock that door before you head up too."

"Night Aunty, thank you." Sybil clutched her note, as though it were trying to escape; firmly and protectively. She knew the words he had chosen for her would be declarations of love. They radiated from the tatty paper, even before her eyes read them and her brain devoured them.

SIXTEEN

"You know the big house has been requisitioned? Well, Ward, staying in Cirencester she is. You know she went to stay with her sick sister? Well, while she was away, Grant did a runner with the family silver!" Aunty Vi chirped as she poured their weak tea from the plump teapot.

Sybil pushed the last image of Grant from her mind. She would forever be stained by his traitor blood on her face.

"You're still so pale my love." Aunty Vi cupped Sybil's face in her hands and studied it with concern.

"I'm ok, really. A little out of sorts, I guess. We still need to put together the next step of our plan for Jeremiah."

WHEN WAR CAME TO LAUNDRY COTTAGE by Sarah Colliver

Sybil accepted the tea which Aunty pushed into her hand and sighed.

"I wondered if we could get one of the local farmers to put an offer together for him, to work for them. Trouble is, on top of the colour issue, he's injured and limited to what he can do." Aunty Vi pursed her lips.

Sybil winced at the thought of colour being any issue, and although she knew this was the way of the world, she would never be able to tolerate it, and certainly not accept it. Perhaps she was still naïve, but no one would be able to convince her otherwise. Jeremiah was a polite, handsome man. He was handy, and hard-working, yes. All those things and so much more. Colour was irrelevant. And anyone who thought otherwise must be crazy, delusional, and ignorant, because why should that matter? Thoughts bubbled inside and flushed her cheeks.

"You got a little colour back, must be the tea. Keep drinking up, and I will cut you a wedge of bread."

Sybil felt strange, as though she was skirting the room, watching her body sat on the little scruffy chair staring at the fire. "Bobby. Bobby Bradford."

Aunty spun on her heels. "Where? Not here?"

"Nope, I saw him with Norman, at the farm. I wasn't snooping, I happened to be passing and caught sight, that's all."

"Passing? It's a dead-end Sybil? The road ends at their farm."

"Yes, it does, you're right. I was having a moment and found myself running. It was my mind, working things out, I hadn't even realised I was running, until I reached the farm. And then I saw the car, and heard voices and it was Norman and Bobby, so I hid. I don't know why, only I didn't want them to see me."

"Norman. With Bobby? Never." Aunty Vi wrung her hands on her apron, her head shook slowly. "What do you suppose they were talking about?"

"I couldn't hear."

WHEN WAR CAME TO LAUNDRY COTTAGE by Sarah Colliver

"I don't believe he would get involved! Too much to lose and he's done a good job of hiding it, because I've not heard a peep of suspicion from anyone."

"That could be to our advantage?"

"How? I don't want no dealings with the black market, no one is going to put my name alongside that kind of thing." Aunty Vi wagged her finger.

"Well, if we had a gentle word about the facts we are in possession of, with Norman, and agreed that we would not reveal anything about what we know, he might be able to find a suitable position for Jeremiah."

"Blackmail?" Auntys' wide eyes, full of shock, would have shamed Sybil a month ago. But after her last few days, and what was at stake with Jeremiah, she barely flinched.

"Don't label it so. I am not trying to get money off him, or do it vindictively, we are simply letting him know that we are aware, and will keep his secret, and he should be so grateful that he will offer us a favour in return. I look on it more as a trade. Not blackmail."

Aunty stared at the floor, as though her mind re-calculated the idea on offer. "When you put it that way, it don't seem quite so nasty. Because, I think a lot of Norman, and would never gossip about him anyway, so we would be reassuring him that his secret is safe. And you think his gratitude would lead to a returned favour?" She nodded. "Yes, that is an acceptable way to go. I would be comfortable with that."

Sybil smiled. Her vision cleared and she sunk into her chair. "So, part one we have a plan for. I would love to get this part done, before our next hospital trip, that would give him hope."

"Well, get that washing in and folded, and the chicken coop cleaned out, whilst you think about approaching Norman. You have until tomorrow night, that's when Sister is back on duty."

Sybil sprung from the chair and kissed Aunty Vi." We make a wonderful team, don't we?"

WHEN WAR CAME TO LAUNDRY COTTAGE by Sarah Colliver

Aunty Vi nodded and wiped her eye with her handkerchief. "Now get on with it before I take this broom to your arse!"

The walk to Norman's farm felt four times the length, from the day she encountered his clandestine meeting with black marketeer, Bobby. This was on account that she was more 'with it' on this occasion and had such an important mission to accomplish. Words swam in her head, and she fought to keep a clear mind. She didn't want to come across as anything but a concerned neighbour. One who needed help, as much as he would need her to keep quiet. She took a deep breath, and reassured herself that if she could cope with a man's brain, splattering across her face and still drive a car, then this was nothing. It was the stakes which were high, keeping Jeremiah here. She pushed that thought from her mind. One step at a time.

She wandered through the rickety old gate, up the path where the farmhouse stood, rather than along the muddy main entrance to the barns. It was 2pm, and she hoped to catch him on a tea break. Norman lived alone and was generally well thought of in the area. His reputation would be important to maintain, and this was in her favour.

"Sybil? Everything ok? Violet alright? Don't usually see you around here?"

"Norman! I hoped to catch you. I have something important to ask to be honest."

"Come in, the pot should still be warm, as I've only just finished a cuppa."

Sybil was surprised as he encouraged her through the front door, by the tidiness of the hallway. Everything had a place, and although the décor was a little shabby in parts, the house was clean and organised.

"Thank you, lovely."

"Is it firewood? Because I feel terrible, I haven't dropped any up to Violet for ages. Time seems to have got away with me. Here, wet, and warm." He passed her a delicate porcelain cup and saucer full to the brim with tea. It appeared to be actual tea, as opposed to the murky liquid they were used to at Laundry Cottage.

"Thank you."

"My wife's favourite." He nodded towards the cup and saucer. "Always gave it to any visitors. A little tradition I have kept, since, well ever since then."

"I'm honoured, it's beautiful." Sybil fought the twinges of guilt which crept into her mind. She had not had much interaction with Norman previously, and he seemed as sweet as Aunty had described. She reminded herself that she wasn't there to blackmail, more to trade.

"Sit, please, and let me know how I can help you and if I can, then I will."

Sybil perched on the edge of a carver chair and placed her tea on the table. "What I am going to tell you, is a bit of a secret...but Aunty assures me, that we can trust you, so..."

"Yes, she knows it."

"We have someone we care for very much. And we want to help him, to stay here with us...only there are reasons why he can't. One of which..." The words stuck in her throat.

"He is black?"

Sybil gasped. "How do you know?"

"I'd rather not say."

"Does everyone know?" Sybil panicked; her mouth felt dry.

"Don't think so. Not heard anyone else is talking about it."

Silence hung in the air. Sybil sipped her tea, which soothed her parched throat; unsure how to proceed.

"Delicious tea, ours is no better than dishwater. Have to reuse it for days." Perhaps he was able to get more, because of his connections, she thought.

"There's enough for another in the pot, give you time to let me know what you are here for. I know you must be after something because you haven't been up before."

Sybil cleared her throat, "Ok then, well I would be most grateful if you could find a position here, on your farm, for Jeremiah to come and work."

"And why would I do that? He's a cripple now I hear, what use would he be to me? I've nothing against the lad, it's terrible what he's been through, and by the hand of his own country men, but I can't go giving jobs to people who can bring nothing to my business. Nothing but trouble in this case." He removed is battered cap and scratched his thinning hair.

She needed to start gentle, imply rather than accuse. "Would anyone you know be able to help?"

"I don't feel as though I could start asking around about him, from the little I know, he's being helped along, if you get my drift but that's not common knowledge and the more attention is drawn his way, the worse his outcome. You mind who you go talking to about him."

"I thought, maybe Bobby Bradford might be useful, he could have some 'low key' ideas or contacts?"

Norman flushed and flipped his cap back onto his head. "No idea, wouldn't give him the time of day."

Sybil stared at him, until he caught her glance and shook his head.

"I saw you Norman, I know he comes here. Aunty Vi and me, we would never gossip about you, Aunty Vi thinks the world of you, and she refused to believe that you had any dealings with Bobby. But being the helpful, community minded soul you are, we thought you would be keen to help us."

"The pot's gone cold now, and I must get on. My farm don't get run from my kitchen, jabbering to you."

Sybil stood. "Thanks for the tea."

"Welcome lass. And I heard what you said. Let me think on it. Tell Vi I will be along this week with a pile of wood for her."

WHEN WAR CAME TO LAUNDRY COTTAGE by Sarah Colliver

Sybil left behind a pensive Norman. She would need to wait for a reaction and hoped it wouldn't take too long because time was ticking for Jeremiah.

Sister McMahon waited at the door as usual and ushered them in through a maze of wards and corridors, to what felt like the deepest depths of the hospital. Her speedy walk, which at times was tricky to keep up with, ensured they were delivered swiftly with minimum fuss to their waiting patient. Poor Aunty Vi's short legs worked in double time, and she was out of puff as they arrived. She slumped against the wall to catch her breath. Sybil did not wait, not wanting to waste a single moment with Jeremiah.

"Here she is." His smile lit up his face, which was healing and almost back to before. A few scabs remained, but the swelling had dissolved. "You've made me feel better already."

"I've only been here for a second!" She hurried to his bed and kissed his face all over, before gently lingering on his mouth.

"You smell like flowers, beautiful. Nothing but disinfectant in here."

"Well, I'm thankful for that because it saved your life, well helped to anyway. Here, Aunty Vi made you this." Sybil placed the lettuce sandwich, wrapped in paper, next to his bed.

"She not with you? How did you get here? Not alone?" Concern crumpled his face.

"She's recovering through that door, all out of puff, but I expect it is really so we can do this." Sybil pressed her lips to his and as she kissed him deeply, her body caught fire and she longed for more.

Jeremiah pushed her away. "Stop, this isn't right, your Aunty Vi could come in at any moment." But he pulled her back into his chest and tucked a strand of hair behind her ear. "Our time will come."

Sybil fought rejection, which was replaced by relief as Aunty Vi arrived, wiping her eye with her handkerchief. "You look better! Now let me see you."

WHEN WAR CAME TO LAUNDRY COTTAGE by Sarah Colliver

"Thank you for coming to see me again, I am so lucky to have you both in my corner." Jeremiah squeezed Sybil's hand.

"Sister says you are making a good recovery, and the operation so far, is promising, which may even mean you have some use of your hand."

"Did she just tell you that? That's incredible, oh I'm so happy, this is the best outcome we could have hoped for." Sybil could barely speak through her joyful tears.

"We aren't out of the woods yet though. She said that there have been lots of questions asked about you. By men in uniforms." Aunty Vi wrung her hands.

Jeremiah sighed. "I wasn't going to say anything about that. To be honest with you both, I'm surprised they've left me alone for this long."

Sybil's emotions swung wildly. Her joy soon turned to panic, and she fought the urge to slump to the floor in despair.

"Well, we have a few ideas, already got the ball rolling, haven't we love?" Aunty Vi turned to Sybil and shot her the 'buck up' look. "Yes, you can count on us, we are going to get you out of here, and bring you home to Laundry cottage to properly recuperate."

The heavy atmosphere forced nervous smiles onto each of their faces, and stifled further chatter, as they pondered their own harboured fears of failure.

SEVENTEEN

Sybil dropped the shopping onto the stony path and rubbed her frozen hands. She cursed her forgotten gloves and lifted the wicker basket up onto her arm. If she picked up pace, she could be back in the warmth of the kitchen within ten minutes. Her mind wandered to past events, where was Harriet now? Was she even alive? What about Walt? She shuddered. It was hard to believe everything she had been through. Sometimes it felt like a dream, other times it was clear and playing out in her mind in technicolour. So much for being sent to the safety of the countryside.

WHEN WAR CAME TO LAUNDRY COTTAGE by Sarah Colliver

On rounding the corner to the lane where Laundry Cottage sat, she watched a distant figure leave the garden and head away, was it Norman? She ran home and flung herself through the kitchen door. "Was it Norman? What did he say?"

Aunty Vi was busy gutting two rabbits. Sybil's eyes darted around the kitchen, where a new stack of kindling sat by the fire.

"He brought these rabbits for us, that there kindling, and some logs being dropped later."

"And?"

"He'll help."

Although Sybil felt immediate relief, something was off. Usually, Aunty Vi would have been waiting at the gate, unable to contain her news. Why was she having to ask her even? "That's amazing, isn't it?"

"Yes. I think it is." Aunty Vi continued the bloody process with expert control, focussing intently.

"What's going on?"

"Well just because he can make an offer of a job, isn't the end of it. It is a start. But he isn't safe, until we get permission from high up. And I don't know how. Norman mentioned that even his 'contacts' refused to touch this because it is so inflammatory. They can get hold of documents, never thought I would be saying this, faked documents, but not when they would be seen by so many officials. The permission needs to be from all the way at the top, and so they'd spot fakes a mile off. He needs a medical discharge, and documents which would allow him to stay here, but we can't even begin to tackle the marriage part, as they simply won't allow negro soldiers to marry us. Even the ones who've fathered children here." She wiped her bloodied hands on her apron and banged her fist on the table. "I don't know which way to turn. Put that kettle on and let's get some fresh tea out, I think we need it."

Sybil mindlessly put together the tea tray amidst a heavy air of contemplation. Both women, caught in their own spiral of despair, chasing ideas and thoughts. They supped their hot tea. "What about Walt? He would have contacts." She caught any further comments from slipping out, remembering to be careful not to imply he was any more than a high rank in the US military. But he wasn't around anymore, his mission accomplished, he would be working on something else. And she had no way of contacting him. She would never get in through the security of whatever place she had been held. That's if she could remember where it was.

"He wouldn't hold enough clout love, he can't fight his country's laws."

"He was our chance, do you think Sister McMahon would have any contacts, or that she is simply a decent citizen who refuses to abide by the segregation rules?" Perhaps she had contact with Walt?

"I think it's more likely her being a good person, God knows we need more of them in the world. No more than that, can't be any more than that to it."

Sybil nodded and sipped on her tea, if only she could talk to Aunty about it all. The rhythmic ticking of the clock and the warmth of the fire made her eyes heavy, and she carefully put her cup on the table. Aunty VI was already dozing in her chair, recent events taking their toll on the two women.

Sybil's dream was a twist of memories, reality, and fear, with Jeremiah being yanked from his hospital bed, and carted away to a dockyard, for shipping home. Taken away as a thing rather than a man. He was trying to show her something, but she couldn't make it out...and then she was back with Walt, sat across a desk, waiting, and Walt slid a packet of cigarettes across the table to her. There was a banging sound, what did it mean? And then she woke and realised it was the front door. She sprung to her feet passed a waking Aunty Vi and at the door stood Sister McMahons son again, with a small brown envelope. He handed it to Sybil and left, pedalling fast up the lane back towards the village.

She tore open the envelope:

Our patient is in imminent danger. They have ordered us to prepare him to travel and are collecting him at 17.00 hours today. I have done my best to stop this, but no luck. Do not come, you will endanger him further. I wanted you to know. Sister M.

WHEN WAR CAME TO LAUNDRY COTTAGE by Sarah Colliver

"NO NO NO!" Sybil screamed as she slammed the door.

"What is it?"

Sybil ran around the front room like a caged animal, unable to verbalise the panic which swamped her.

"What is it girl?" Aunty Vi grabbed her hard. "Stop this now." She snatched the note and read it. "Right, we need to think."

Sybil remembered her dream and ran upstairs to find the dress and jacket she wore the night of the shooting. She yanked them from the wardrobe, and threw them onto her bed, frantically searching the pockets. "Please, please, please," she murmured as she felt a bulge and inhaled deeply, aware that this could be the thing that somehow gave them a chance. She pulled out the cigarette pack that Walt had left that night, there was one cigarette left, and she ran back downstairs carrying the precious cargo.

Aunty Vi stood clutching the crumple note in silence, watching her circle the room.

WHEN WAR CAME TO LAUNDRY COTTAGE by Sarah Colliver

Sybil struck a match and lit the cigarette, inhaling deeply and wrestling with her rising fear. What was it, what about it? What did it mean? It was simply an ordinary cigarette packet, nothing unusual at all. She pounded her forehead with her palm. She examined the outside of the box; nothing. Then felt inside with her fingertips, which extracted a tiny piece of paper:

WHI 0452 ask for Louise.

"I knew it! I knew he wouldn't let us down!"

"Have you lost your mind? What's going on? Put that cigarette out."

"I can't tell you much. But this, this is our way forward, now I must run to the telephone box, please tell me we have pennies?"

"I'm lost and have no idea what on earth is going on now, but I do trust you girl. Get the tin down from the high shelf, the old tea tin up there, should be coins in there."

Sybil took five, in case, and ran out of the house and up the lane, but the telephone box was occupied, and her heart sank at the sight of two others awaiting their turn. "Excuse me, I am sorry to ask, but can I go next, we're having an emergency, and I have no time to waste?"

"I don't mind," replied the elderly gentleman with a smile. "Are you ok?"

"I mind! We've all got emergencies of our own love, there is a war on."

The kind old man gently pulled Sybil in front of him, so that she headed the small queue, and shot a look of disdain at the moaning woman. "It's obvious something important is happening here, look at her! So, show some compassion, war or not."

The moaning lady sighed and turned her back on them, but he reassuringly squeezed Sybil's arm. "Hope you get sorted out my love," he said as she jumped into the box, barely allowing the previous occupant to leave.

"Steady on love!" He said as he wandered away shaking his head.

WHEN WAR CAME TO LAUNDRY COTTAGE by Sarah Colliver

Sybil felt sick as she grabbed the receiver pushed in four pennies and dialled the number. She pushed the button as the voice spoke, "Hello."

"Can I speak to Louise please?" She managed to say.

"One moment."

Sybil readied another coin, desperate for the call not to disconnect.

"Connecting you now," the clipped voice advised.

"Sybil?"

"How do you know it's me?"

"Because you asked for Louise."

"That makes sense. Walt, I need your help. Desperately." The pips beeped, "Hold on!" She pushed another coin into the slot.

"I know, you wouldn't be phoning otherwise, and I can guess who it involves."

"They're taking him, tonight! Sister McMahon can't stop them. I don't know what to do. I have work for

WHEN WAR CAME TO LAUNDRY COTTAGE by Sarah Colliver

him, a local farmer, but we have no documents, he needs discharge papers and some kind of dispensation to stay?"

Walt cleared his throat. "I told you from the start this was doomed, you and him."

"I didn't call for a lecture, I need your help. You told me I saved your life, and although I hate to say it, that means you owe me."

"I also told you that I am one man, I cannot fight the law. But let me see what I can do. I have connections this side of the water, who may be more sympathetic and call in a favour or two. I must go, and I can promise nothing. Goodbye Sybil."

The telephone line went dead, and the growing queue outside grumbled as she left. The elderly gentleman smiled before taking his turn.

She chewed her nails all the way home, trying to figure out what was going to happen, and utterly despairing of her situation. Her weary legs felt like lead, and she inched along at a snail's pace. Numbness crept through her body like dark shadows. Could she risk getting to the hospital? She needed to see him, and yet, the last time she had been so selfish and naïve, put him there, battered and left for dead.

"You seen a ghost?" Aunty Vi said. She was wrapped up in her coat and head scarf, waiting at the gate. "Did the call not go well?"

Sybil shuffled past her and out the back of the house to the empty side of vegetable patch. She grabbed a spade and began to dig. The ground was hard with frost, and with every cut of the soil, and jolt of the spade, her hands became more painful. Aunty Vi watched on from the kitchen door.

"My lovely girl, it's been half an hour, and you haven't come up for breath or said one word. Put the spade in the shed and come on in the warm now, before you catch your death. And I won't take no for an answer. I don't often boss you around, because you don't often need it, but right this moment, if I have to come out there and drag your arse in, I will."

Sybil turned to Aunty Vi, who stood with her hands on her hips and a stern face. She was anything but scary and made her giggle. Laughter bubbled up from her sickened core until she was doubled over, and unable to stop. It was the type of sound, not happy or silly, but chilling and hysterical.

"Right, that's it." Aunty Vi swept her broom into the air and spanked Sybil's bottom. "You stop this now," she shouted.

Sybil unfolded until she was upright and her face stone. The spade fell to the freshly turned soil, and they both trudged away into the kitchen, where Aunty Vi pushed her into the chair nearest the fire and threw a blanket onto her.

"Think we both need a brandy, here drink this. It'll warm you as quick as tea. Things always work themselves out, and sometimes things are out of our hands, and we can't make it right, life doesn't always give us what we want. But that poor man, what will he be sent back to? What life will he have? Oh…" Aunty Vi wiped her tears away.

"I don't know anything anymore. Walt said he may be able to help, but no promise given. I can't go to the hospital, I daren't. I was the one who put him there by being selfish. My legs are threatening to carry me there, and I must physically stop them, because I fear once I leave that gate, I won't have any control."

"Well, that's what love does for you. You put them first. And even though this is the hardest thing you have ever done, staying away, you have done so to protect him. I'm proud of you, girl."

Sybil wept. Deep racking, messy wails. Her heavy heart broke at the thought of Jeremiah being carted away, by a mob of men who hate him, not because he was evil, or sadistic, or untrustworthy, but because they could only see colour and nothing beyond. It was so unfair, that not only was he to fight against the common enemy, but amongst his hateful allies. He was surrounded by blood thirsty war mongers, who kill without any regard for life. What a sorry state the world was in.

EIGHTEEN

"Well, we have work to do. There's a war on. People come and go, live or die, but food must be provided, land has to be worked and life carries on, my girl. It sounds cruel, hard, but we don't get a pass to fall apart. Look at all those I have lost, my own flesh and blood, and do you see me holed up in my bed?"

Sybil nodded as guilt pecked at her, she knew she was slacking. Her low mood, affected Aunty, and how selfish was she, wallowing in her own pity and anger, when Aunty Vi had thrown herself into helping her try and save Jeremiah? She suspected that because this was so soon after the loss of Robert, it was in his honour. "I know. Everyone has lost someone, but I feel so empty. It's as if the meaning has been sucked out of my life."

"Well, that's grief love. And we all must find our way out of it."

Their conversations seem to be on a loop, snatched in between jobs as Aunty Vi cajoled her into one more task.

"Three days! Nothing! If they'd taken him, Sister would have sent word, if they hadn't, we would be able to visit? It's the not knowing which is killing me."

"Now listen, across the whole of the world right now, people don't know if their loved ones are alive or not, but it still turns, at this point no one has the luxury of collapsing because of a lack of information. I hate to be so stern with you, but you gotta get a grip girl. You need to stiffen up your resolve, and find that steely determination which you have, I know it, I seen it. I need you. You don't know what you gave me when you came to stay. It was as if I was waiting to die, and you brought me the chance of a new life. We are in this together, but you must buck up."

Sybil nodded again. "You're right, I'm being selfish. Sorry."

Little Aunty Vi pulled her into a warm embrace, "Onwards, right? Together."

Sybil took three deep breaths and vowed to pull herself together, as a knock on the front door broke their mood, and both women stood and stared with paled faces. It was as though they were frozen in time, and neither moved. The door knocked again, and Sybil took Aunty's hand as they headed to the door together.

"Ladies. Can I come in?" Sister McMahon looked exhausted, and the lines carved into her face evidenced the tough job she performed relentlessly. Sybil's guilt at her own self-pity flushed her face, in the presence of this woman, who seemed as though she hadn't slept for the entire war.

"Come in, sit down. Would you like a tea?"

"Thank you, I would." Sister McMahon sat and crossed her legs.

"Did you walk all this way?" Aunty Vi tried to be chirpy amidst the heavy atmosphere.

"Only from the village. It was actually a pleasant walk, amongst the hedgerows and birds. Don't get to see much of nature in the hospital." She sipped on her tea and Sybil leant against the door frame, desperate for news, but too afraid to ask. Silence.

WHEN WAR CAME TO LAUNDRY COTTAGE by Sarah Colliver

Sister McMahon slowly placed her cup on the side table. "I'll get straight to the point. I'm afraid our patient passed away yesterday."

Sybil's hands flew to her gaping mouth, and she slid down the wall to the floor. Aunty Vi's hand wobbled as she put down her own cup, but she managed to compose herself enough to ask, "How, when he was doing so well?"

"Infection I'm afraid. Post operative. That was the reason he needed to stay under our care for the full six weeks, with his arm covered. If it is any comfort at all, it was calm and relatively peaceful."

"Well, that lad deserved some peace, I reckon, and can't be harmed no more. Sybil, get up and get the candle, let's light it for him. Put it here on the table. Sybil! Don't you go creeping down that lane of self-pity again. Before you start going on about it, it wasn't your fault. He was a grown man who must have thought you were worth the risk. You didn't force him to that dance, whether you coaxed him into it or not. He could have said no."

WHEN WAR CAME TO LAUNDRY COTTAGE by Sarah Colliver

Sister McMahon leaned across and thoughtfully sipped her tea. "The snippets of chatter we shared, was the joy meeting you, brought him. He told me that you meant everything to him. You gave him hope, and that what he thought was impossible, could somehow be..."

Sybil dissected her words. She kept the ones which would get her through and clung to them. "Thank you for all you did for him. At least he must have felt there were kind people here, that were on his side. Even if we didn't manage to save him." Her chest felt as though it were being crushed, and her voice could only manage a whisper.

Sybil placed the candle, which burned not so long ago for Aunty Violet's losses, on the table and lit it, as the other two women watched.

"To a wonderful man, who will be missed." Aunty Vi spoke tearfully and stood, followed by Sister McMahon. They each raised their teacups to the burning candle, and Sybil swallowed the torrent of grief which she could never allow to erupt.

WHEN WAR CAME TO LAUNDRY COTTAGE by Sarah Colliver

SEPTEMBER 1945

Sybil and Aunty Vi linked arms, and headed home, from the village. Their brandy induced high spirits, were tainted with loss. The collective grief of their village was evident, despite the cheers and smiles and victorious songs, the toasts to those lost were poignant and sobering. With so many lives eradicated, Sybil felt the high price which brought victory, from her core. It was hard to celebrate when the losses were unimaginable numbers. Still, the red, white, and blue bunting fluttered across the square, and criss-crossed the main road from every window. Flags hung from each available receptacle and every doorstep was occupied by chattering women, whose moods swung wildly between tears of relief and devastation. As though they had been brave for so long, that now the line was drawn, the war really was ended, it all came flooding to the surface.

The World War was over and yet, the personal war, brought to her by Private Jeremiah Thomas, still raged. The friendly enemy, deemed as heroes, still enforced segregation and injustice occurred daily on the streets of America. It felt like no one cared about this, but it simmered in her gut and threatened to send her insane with anger.

"I think we should have one more tot of brandy when we get back, and maybe a hunk of bread, and jam. What do you think?"

"Well, I think we've probably had enough, you're a bad influence on me Aunty."

They giggled and Sybil squeezed her arm.

"Yes, I am, for today at least…what I really want to do, is our own little toast to those we have loved and lost."

"Absolutely, I would be honoured to part-ip-i-cate…" Sybil hiccupped, "I mean part-ic-ipate."

They turned into their lane, and Sybil stopped for a moment, she wanted to breathe it all in. The war had brought her to this place, and she never wanted to leave. Her eyes darted from the wild hedgerows, and dry-stone walls, to the rolling fields which stretched out as far as the disappearing horizon, beneath the light of the huge moon. How she wished for one last kiss with Jeremiah, beneath it.

The local GIs were gone now, and although she knew Jeremiah was dead, it felt as though their leaving took him too. Silly. So many had no body, or grave to tend and mourn at. She and Aunty Vi planted up a flower bed down near the brook. Between them, they carried the rickety old bench which had always lived by the kitchen door, there, so they could sit and listen to the babble of the brook and remember. There was room enough for them to sit together when they would share thoughts or memories. But also, a space for private grief. Sybil had rubbed off the splintery edges, smoothed it down, and painted it with a tin of sticky old remnants, donated by Norman, who had continued to watch out for Aunty Vi. Bringing occasional treats as well as a steady supply of wood and rabbit.

"Right, you go and sit on our bench, and I'll sort out the brandy." Aunty Vi headed into the kitchen, with a wobbly skip.

WHEN WAR CAME TO LAUNDRY COTTAGE by Sarah Colliver

Sybil sat down. The gentle brook soothed her, and the bright night sky felt powerful, as though it was trying to heal the world. She bathed her face in moonlight and felt grateful that Jeremiah was at peace, because she could never have rested not knowing what he was experiencing, back home in America.

"Here girl." Aunty Vi handed a brandy to her.

"That's more than a tot!"

"Well, between us we got a few to remember, only fitting. Look at that moon, it's a beauty tonight."

"Aren't we lucky? To have each other. You know how much I love you, can I stay here with you, always?"

Aunty Vi wiped her eye with her handkerchief and nodded. "I hoped you would, because you are as much a daughter to me as I could wish for, only I you're my friend too. I couldn't bear it if you left, but I didn't want you to feel obliged."

"Told you before, you and me, we make an amazing team. And I honestly am so at home here, with you. I will write to Mum and Dad tomorrow, I think they may come and see us, now the war is over completely."

"Oh, talking of notes, this was left for us." She whipped a handwritten note from her pocket.

Dear Vi & Sybil

Please come for tea at the farm tomorrow, at 3pm. No need to bring anything, just your company, which I am very much looking forward to.

Warm regards, Norman

"He wants to marry you!"

"Don't be foolish girl, we admire each other, and I think the world of him, but both of us are too long in the tooth for any of those shenanigans. Don't be thinking such thoughts. It's his way of marking the end of the war, tis all."

"We'll see! I hear wedding bells…"

"Shush, that's not why we are here." Aunty Vi stood and lifted her glass up to the moon, followed by Sybil.

WHEN WAR CAME TO LAUNDRY COTTAGE by Sarah Colliver

"To those we love, who we were privileged to love and have their love back, who made us better people in their time on earth, who we shall never forget, and who will remain in our hearts forever. Cheers to you all."

"To you all."

Sybil carried the basket, although Norman said to bring nothing, they couldn't turn up empty handed, and so they picked the two plumpest lettuces, and their last jar of hedgerow jam.

"I was surprised at how tidy and clean Norman keeps his house when I visited. Considering he has a farm to run too."

"Mable was a house-proud woman, and he was devastated when she passed. Vowed to keep it how she would have wanted and kept his word. He's a man of his word is Norman."

They reached the gate, which seemed to be recently mended and no longer scraped on the ground, and beneath the front window hung two smart window boxes. "He's been sprucing this place up. Reckon he's making it more appealing for a love interest."

Aunty Vi stopped in her tracks. "I'm not joking now girl, you stop this, because it's embarrassing, and we are now and will only ever be friends. So, sort your silly head out and stop saying these things, or I shall turn around and go home."

Sybil blushed. "Sorry. I promise, no more." Aunty rarely spoke so sternly, and she had gone too far. She silently followed her to the door, where a smart Norman stood waiting to greet his guests.

"Ladies, you are as lovely as ever. Please come in."

"Thank you, brought you this as a token of our appreciation, and don't refuse it or I shall be offended and leave." Aunty Vi handed him their gifts proudly.

"Well, that is kind, thank you we shall enjoy the jam." Norman took the produce and placed it on the kitchen table. "Do go through to the parlour."

"Ooh, thank you." Sybil smiled.

WHEN WAR CAME TO LAUNDRY COTTAGE by Sarah Colliver

A pristine white tablecloth covered the table, and the best porcelain and table wear, which could only ever have been used on a few occasions, was spread across it. "We may still be at the mercy of rationing, but we can enjoy this legacy of Mable's today."

"How thoughtful, it all looks beautiful. Thank you. But you seem to have laid an extra place." Aunty Vi puzzled.

"Oh yes! I forgot, I need to introduce you to my house guest, well I say house guest, but he's been here for some time! Please come in – this is Mr Thomas Pearson.

Sybil and Aunty Vi stared towards the door, waiting for a glance of the mysterious house guest.

"Ladies, I am pleased to meet you."

A silence of disbelief held them captive for what felt like eternity, as they fought to process his arrival with open mouths.

"Jeremiah! How? Is it you? I..." Sybil's croaky voice broke, and her eyes pooled with tears. "But you died? They cremated you..."

She stood up, her eyes fixated on him and sought answers to the many questions darting around her mind. Jeremiah took her hand and pulled her in close to him. His warm body enveloped her, and she clung to his tall frame, she was home again. He smelled of soap and her body instantly awoke with his touch. Sybil could not verbalise her tangled thoughts, but she knew that in his arms was exactly where she belonged.

Aunty Vi wiped her eyes with her hanky, and Norman handed her a whiskey. "Think we could all do with one of these."

"Well, that was a secret well kept, and so close by too." She chinked her glass with Norman's and then in unison they knocked back their drink. "Let's give them a moment, shall we have a wander outside?"

Norman refilled their glasses and nodded." Good idea, I think these two need a little time alone. Come on Vi.

WHEN WAR CAME TO LAUNDRY COTTAGE by Sarah Colliver

I will show you all the jobs my new house guest has been doing to stave off his melancholy, waiting for the war to end."

Aunty Vi followed him out into the garden, pulling the parlour door closed behind her.

Sybil lifted her head up to Jeremiah's face. His velvet voice soothed her ears, "I've been dreaming of kissing you for a long time, my love. You have occupied my thoughts ever since I was in hospital, you made me believe, dare to hope for more." He sat in the chair and pulled her onto his lap. Her arms slipped up around his neck and she kissed him deeply, from her inner core, she committed herself to him, forever. Her body sought his touch and she ached for more, as his fingertips trailed her neck and back.

"My Sybil, we can be married now, if you're still sure you want to. I mean it's no easy path ahead if you agree to be my wife, Mrs Pearson."

"How could you doubt it? I've lost you once already, I'm not letting you go again, not ever." She pecked at his cheeks and forehead. "How, I mean, I still don't understand...you died, they cremated you?"

"Our Sister McMahon, an angel that woman. She had the idea of injecting me with poison, enough to make me ill, but not enough to kill me." Jeremiah brushed his lips over her hand, his eyes fixed on hers. "When my military escort came to repatriate me, they found me burning up with a contagious disease, at death's door. Sister said they weren't keen to get too close. They left, and lucky for me, reported back that I was dying. So, when the hospital provided a certificate of cremation, they asked no more questions."

"She must have been getting help from someone."

"They gave me a new identity, our friend Walter Raslow had a hand in this I believe."

Sybil smiled. So, Walt had come through for them after all. Perhaps he was more involved in this entire rescue, than she realised.

"They got me well enough to travel and then transported me in a delivery truck here. Once I was well enough, I started to help around the place and waited. I hid if anyone came by."

Sybil kissed him again. "You were so close by, all this time."

"It drove me mad to think I could almost hear your voice on the wind, and not see you. But it also got me through, knowing we breathed the same air and felt the same rain on our skin. I sure learned patience, waiting for today."

Aunty Vi knocked on the parlour door and Norman followed her inside.

"Vi, Sybil, Thomas, I wish to make a toast if I may?" Here take one of these each." He handed out the last of the whiskey, and they all stood up with their glasses raised. Sybil held onto Jeremiah's arm carefully.

"To victory, peace, and to us four- stood here now, because it takes courage to stand up for what you believe in. To put your own neck on the line for another. We fought our own battle here, in our little corner of the countryside, and by God we won." Norman's lip quivered as he spoke.

WHEN WAR CAME TO LAUNDRY COTTAGE by Sarah Colliver

Sybil rested her eyes on each person in the room for a second. Her life was unrecognisable now, compared to the one she left behind in the city. The bomb which she narrowly escaped in the factory, which killed her friends and threw her family into premature grief, had propelled her to the very spot where she now stood.

How strange life could be, and how wonderful too, she thought, as she stared up at her handsome man, content in the knowledge he was safe, and he was finally hers.

WHEN WAR CAME TO LAUNDRY COTTAGE by Sarah Colliver

Thoughts:

240,000 African American GIs were stationed in the UK, over a three-year period of the second world war.

James Grigg, Secretary for State for War- "It is undesirable that there should be any unnecessary association between American coloured troops and British women, whether civilian or in the forces." – extract from 'United States Coloured Troops in the UK document.'

A West Country Farmer- "I love Americans, but I don't like those white ones that they've bought with them."

Source: Mixedmuseum.org.uk

WHEN WAR CAME TO LAUNDRY COTTAGE by Sarah Colliver

With Special thanks to:

Emma Gazzard for creating this beautiful cover and encouraging me to keep writing. **Elaine Malsom** for sharing her wonderful stories about the real Laundry Cottage & for listening to me over and over, spilling my ideas. **Rachel Norman** for being a tower of strength and support, despite her own battles. **Melanie Maguire** for her eagle eyes & encouragement not to give up. And my lush cousin **Lynsey Walker**, who always tells me how it is, loves me for who I am, and took me back in time to Beamish.

Sarah Colliver is the author of 'In Deep' & 'Deeper Still', a two-book series, set high in the Spanish mountains. If you enjoy a dramatic, sexy, and gritty storyline, these books are for YOU. Her third book, 'We Close our Eyes' is set in a sleepy English village, where secrets and lies will ultimately undo three lives. No one can hide their true self forever.

ALL books are available NOW on Amazon, in paperback and on Kindle.

WHEN WAR CAME TO LAUNDRY COTTAGE by Sarah Colliver

About the Artist:

EMMA GAZZARD is an illustrator based in the Forest of Dean, Gloucestershire. Emma studied illustration, graphic design, and photography for five years, at both Bournemouth and Poole College of Art & Design and Exeter, where she graduated as a Batchelor or Arts. She went on to illustrate freelance over a number of years, and now creates commissions.

Emma has an online shop specialising in designs for products & clothing, influenced by popular culture and kitsch aesthetics.

Shop: zerozombiegirl.redbubble.com

Instagram: emmagazzard_design

Printed in Great Britain
by Amazon